Fabulous
FATHERS

He's more than a man—he's a fabulous father!

Caleb Remmick on Fatherhood:

I've always believed that a man has responsibilities. There are 3,600 people who work for my company. That makes 3,600 families who depend on me to make the right decisions to keep the business going. I want my son to grow up and understand the importance of a man's work.

Josh is a super kid—kind of quiet...mature for his age. When he was born, it was like a light coming on in my soul. I loved him from that first moment, and I love him now.

He understands that I love him and that I'm building something for his future. *He* doesn't complain or accuse me of neglect. However, I know he has a right to expect more from me. I'm trying to make sure I can be there for him. In spite of what Eden thinks, my son is the most important part of my life. I want to be a full-time father to him.

Fabulous
FATHERS

LAURIE PAIGE
Caleb's Son

Silhouette Books

Published by Silhouette Books
America's Publisher of Contemporary Romance

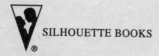

SILHOUETTE BOOKS
®

ISBN-13: 978-0-373-18896-3

Recycling programs
for this product may
not exist in your area.

CALEB'S SON

Visit Silhouette Books at www.eHarlequin.com

Printed in U.S.A.

LAURIE PAIGE

"One of the nicest things about writing romances is researching locales, careers and ideas. In the interest of authenticity, most writers will try anything...once." Along with her writing adventures, Laurie has been a NASA engineer and a past president of the Romance Writers of America. She is also a mother and a grandmother. She was twice a Romance Writers of America RITA® Award finalist for Best Traditional Romance and has won awards from *Romantic Times BOOKreviews* for Best Silhouette Special Edition and Best Silhouette, in addition to appearing on the *USA TODAY* bestseller list. Recently resettled in Northern California, Laurie is looking forward to whatever experiences her next novel will send her on.

Chapter One

"Your résumé says you speak French." Mr. Taft, seated behind the polished walnut desk, was middle-aged and balding. He wore glasses, had a thin mustache and didn't look at all intimidating. In fact, he looked like a stern but kindly uncle.

Eden Sommers smiled her best teacher's smile—calm, assured and in control, which wasn't how she felt at all. "Yes. French was my minor in college. I've taught French, English and literature at the academy the past five years."

All she knew about this job was what her best friend, Sue Harrell, had told her that morning—that the boy was five, almost six, and needed a tutor in English for the summer. Sue had been very excited about the position and had insisted that Eden rush right over to apply. "Just take your résumé and go over. I told the man to expect you—"

"You didn't!" Eden had cried, aghast. She wasn't prepared for a job interview on such short notice.

"So you have to go," her friend had calmly concluded.

"There'll probably be a thousand applicants," Eden had replied, not putting much hope in the possibility of landing such a job. "It sounds like a plum, especially if they're paying what you said. I'll need Mary Poppins to blow the others away."

Sue had laughed. "Maybe she's already cleared a path. Dress up and get over there before anyone else shows up. Wear that white two-piece dress with the gold daisies. It looks wonderful with your eyes. Don't forget the matching earrings."

Eden glanced down at the dress. The white contrasted nicely with her light tan, gained from supervising recess each afternoon. The daisies complemented the sun streaks in her hair and brought out the golden tones in her light brown eyes. The outfit looked okay for business with its fitted jacket and straight skirt.

"The Justine Academy for Young Ladies," Mr. Taft read from her résumé. "You're tenured there and will be returning when the school year resumes in the autumn?"

She stiffened, sensing from his tone that this could be a disadvantage, then forced herself to relax. "Yes."

Her position at the academy was secure. However, due to budget cuts, her summer job as tutor to Chicago's inner-city students had been cancelled at the last minute. That left her personal budget somewhat awry, one might say.

A smile, one that barely touched the corners of her mouth, flickered over her lips at the irony of the situation. She and her mother, who had once had enough money for a lifetime, or so they had thought, now had to count every penny twice.

The man behind the desk frowned, and her nerves clenched again. *Don't look desperate,* she warned herself.

She watched his neat black-and-gray mustache move up

and down as he pursed his lips; then he spoke. "My client may need you longer than the summer."

"Most children can easily become conversant in a language within three months," she stated. "However, I can work with him after school each day for as long as necessary. You said he does know some English?"

The man nodded, the light from the window reflecting from his bald head, which looked healthy and pink. A well-fed, self-satisfied man, she decided, then stopped herself. She had learned long ago not to pass quick judgments on men.

"Hmm," Mr. Taft said.

She realized his job was exactly that—to assess and judge a person from a fifteen-minute interview. She hoped she would pass. She settled back in her chair and tried to appear relaxed, yet alert.

"Your qualifications are excellent." He glanced at a wall clock. "However, my client reserves the right to make the final selection. He should have arrived at the airport ten minutes ago. Are you available for lunch?"

The question startled her. "Uh, yes."

Her heart beat fast with elation. She'd made the final cut! One more hurdle to go. She assumed the client was the father of the boy and wondered briefly about the mother.

Mr. Taft wrote swiftly on a sheet of paper. He put the note, along with her résumé, in an envelope and sealed it. After writing on the envelope, he handed it across the desk to her.

"You'll give this to my client?"

"Of course." She took it from him.

"Reservations have been made at the restaurant," Mr. Taft informed her, and he mentioned an expensive place in a large hotel. When he stood, clearly a dismissal, she did, too. He walked her to the door.

"Thank you for seeing me without an appointment," she said, holding out her hand to him.

They shook hands. A smile curled his lips under the neat mustache. "It was a pleasure. A real pleasure."

A frisson chased along her neck. He seemed so…satisfied. "What name should I ask for?" she thought to ask. "At lunch," she added at his inquiring glance.

"Oh." He beamed at her. "It's on the envelope." He closed the door.

Eden said goodbye to the secretary of the employment agency, noted that there were no other applicants in the office and went out to the elevator.

Riding down to the street level of the skyscraper, she decided Mr. Taft's client must be influential if a headhunter firm that usually dealt at the corporate-vice-president level and above would spend time filling a lowly tutor's position for him. She looked at the envelope to see who the person was.

Her heart stopped, raced, skipped several beats, then raced again. "It can't be," she whispered.

The elevator door opened.

"Are you getting off?" A man's voice intruded on her shock.

She stared at him.

"You okay, lady?" The young man held a vase of flowers. His uniform indicated he was from a local florist's shop. He got on the elevator and pushed the button to hold the door open.

"Uh, yes," she managed to say, stepping into the lobby of the massive office building, one owned by the Remmick Corporation. Her gaze went to the polished granite entrance, where the name was engraved on a brass plaque. Remmick and Son, Inc.

It couldn't be Caleb. Fate wouldn't be so cruel.

For a moment, she leaned against the cool granite and sought the calm she'd learned to exhibit over the years.

When had fate ever been kind? she questioned with a sardonic twist of her lips as she regained her equilibrium.

Besides, the client didn't have to be *Caleb* Remmick. Just because he and his father owned the building didn't necessarily mean a thing. Or the fact that he had a son who should be about six years old. There were other Remmicks in the phone book.

Not many, a worried voice deep inside of her replied. She'd looked up the name in the Chicago directory shortly after they'd met. Of course, Caleb had had an unlisted number.

She swallowed against the knot that formed in her throat. Tears burned harshly in her eyes.

Dear heaven, she was twenty-six years old, not nineteen. She didn't think life was perfect, that love, once given, was forever. By the time she'd turned twenty, she'd known better.

Pulling herself erect, she walked out of the impressive building and down the street to the parking garage. Keeping a sharp eye out for muggers and such, she unlocked her ancient vehicle and climbed inside. In a moment, she was off to meet her destiny. She shook her head at her fatalistic misgivings.

She hit a traffic snarl at once and was reduced to a crawl as she headed toward the freeway. Forty-five minutes later, she arrived at the hotel.

She grimaced as she let the valet park her car. It was money she could ill afford, but she didn't have time to drive around looking for a parking space. Mr. Remmick might be waiting.

Caleb frowned at his watch and took another sip of wine. Taft had said the tutor selected for his son was on her way over. He'd give her one more minute, then he would order. After lunch, he had two meetings before he headed home to talk to his father. Today was Monday. On Thursday, he'd leave on another trip—Washington, D.C., this time—to talk to a Senate committee.

He pressed a hand to his eyes. God, he was tired. He'd just returned from a meeting in Cancún. There'd been a storm that had wiped out half the South American coffee crop, and several planters had tried to renege on contracts they'd previously signed.

Sometimes he wondered what the hell he was doing in the commodities market—coffee, sugar, tea and spices were his specialties—when anything, including real estate and oil, had to pay better and be less hazardous to the nerves.

Too much rain, not enough rain, rain at the wrong time; insects, disease, war, rumors of war—anything could wipe out a year's profits in the blink of an eye.

Once he'd loved the excitement of it—buying and selling, wheeling and dealing, all on a grand scale…at least, he'd thought he'd loved it. Now he wasn't so sure. His work formed the center of his life, but it no longer made his adrenaline flow.

Jet lag, he diagnosed. About twelve years of it. God, but he was tired.

He glanced at his watch again. Where the hell was the woman? "Waiter," he called.

Time was money and it was a-wasting, as his father said. Used to say. The old man had changed since his last stroke.

Caleb sighed. The stroke had occurred sixteen months ago. Life was tougher now. Caleb had to take on more responsibility. He'd been the legs of the company for a long time, rushing to hot spots and putting out fires, troubleshooting their various and far-flung enterprises.

And nothing to come home to, except an empty house, an insidious voice inside him prodded.

He shook his head. Not even that anymore. He'd sold the house in Martinique. It had seemed pointless to keep it after his wife—pretty, gentle Antoinette—had died. For a moment, he felt the regret that always hit him concerning his marriage.

He'd known before a year was up that they'd made a mistake, each of them marrying on the rebound. Worse for Antoinette, he admitted. He'd had his work. She'd had the house and little else, except for fragments of his time. She'd wanted it that way.

Then they'd had Josh.

A fierce tenderness came over him. It often did when he thought of his son. Josh was the reason he was here at a hotel in Chicago, waiting to interview a tutor, instead of rushing off to Washington to take care of business.

Antoinette's parents, who had lived at the house and looked after the boy, wanted to retire to their home village in France. They were willing to take Josh with them, but Caleb had thanked them for their help for the past two years and declined.

He and Josh were going to live at the family abode in Chicago. It was time the child knew of his heritage from his father's side of the family.

The waiter came over to him. Caleb realized there was a woman following the man. He rose to his feet.

The waiter held out the chair opposite him.

"What the hell?" Caleb exclaimed, sitting down abruptly.

"Hello, Caleb," Eden said, managing a pleasant tone.

She took the chair the waiter held for her and let him snap the napkin out of its folds and drop it across her knees before maneuvering her closer to the table. She accepted the menu. When he left, she felt abandoned. It didn't take a genius to recognize the beginnings of fury on Caleb's face.

Her earlier thought had been correct. Fate was never kind. It hadn't been in years. Why should she expect it to be different now?

"I'm waiting for someone," Caleb announced, his voice cold, his eyes blazing.

He still hadn't forgiven her for breaking up with him the night of their engagement party, it seemed. She sorted through her shaky emotions and chose irony for a response. The situation was nothing if not ironic.

"The tutor," she said, forcing a half smile. Her voice was still calm, she was pleased to note. "That's me."

"The hell it is," he said grimly, low enough that his words carried no farther than their table. Around them, other diners were chatting and laughing. Their table was alive with tension.

"I think I'm the only one who applied. People want permanent jobs with medical and retirement benefits nowadays. Only schoolteachers and teenagers have to scramble for summer jobs."

He took a drink from his wineglass. She noticed that his hand trembled slightly. Probably from the strain of not throwing the wine in her face…the way she'd tossed a glass of champagne on him when he'd finally arrived at their party two hours late. She'd told him she never wanted to see him again.

She'd been more dramatic in those days. Since then, she'd learned to be rational. Life had demanded it.

Caleb muttered an expletive, something she'd never heard him say during those idyllic times of yore. Seven years. A lifetime.

"Here," she said, pulling out the envelope and handing it over. She felt like a spy giving out secret documents. Perhaps she should make a run for it now, while she was safe.

Safe? Caleb, no matter how he felt, would hardly attack

her here in public, or private, either, for that matter. No matter how angry he'd been in their mutual past, he'd never once caused her to fear for her safety.

He ripped the letter open. His dark eyes ran over the note, then scanned her résumé. He flicked her a glance that seared like a phosphorous match, it was so hot with fury.

The light from the atrium windows picked out highlights that sparkled like diamond dust in his hair, which was still as black and shiny as a crow's wing. Well, she would hardly have expected him to go gray in seven years. He was…thirty-four? Yes.

Nearly eight years older than she was. When she'd been nineteen, he'd been twenty-seven and already a power to be reckoned with in the city, having taken over for his father, who'd had a stroke that year. Mr. Remmick had had another one early last year, her friend Sue had told her.

"I'm sorry about your father," Eden said. "Is he better?"

"Some." Caleb folded the papers, shoved them into the envelope and stuck them in the inner pocket of his coat.

She suddenly remembered unbuttoning his coat and snuggling inside, loving the feel of his warmth. He'd teased her about women wearing strapless evening dresses even when the wind off the lake was freezing. They'd laughed about the ridiculous fashions…one of the few times they had shared laughter, she recalled.

Other emotions had been so much more compelling—the hunger, the need to see each other, the agony of long-distance calls when his work had taken him out of town, the ecstasy of being with him…and then the hurt and the anger, the arguments over his schedule.

He had worked her into his life in bits and pieces. It hadn't been enough. Not for her. Not for a lifetime.

For a second, tears stung her eyes.

Caleb narrowed his midnight-dark eyes at her. "Tears?" he asked. He was blunt as well as observant.

"No," she denied, blinking them away. She moved in her chair, intending to rise. She wanted to leave before she remembered more, before she lost control of her emotions.

She hadn't realized the meeting would be so difficult. During the traffic jam, she'd thought over what her reactions might be if the client turned out to be Caleb. She had decided she could handle it. She'd even take the job if he offered it.

The waiter appeared. "May I take your order?"

"Yes," Caleb said. He ordered quickly, choosing salad, a main course and coffee without a pause.

The two men looked at her. "I'll have the same," she said, settling into the chair.

The day wouldn't be a complete loss, she decided philosophically. She'd get a meal out of this fiasco if nothing else. For sure, the job was down the tubes.

Lunch was eaten mostly in silence. Eden was aware of Caleb peering at her from time to time, as if trying to figure her out. He probably thought she had some sneaky scheme to win him back and get her hands on his money.

He finished eating and leaned back in the chair, his face impassive. Motioning for the waiter, he indicated his coffee cup.

The waiter refilled both cups, removed their plates and disappeared without a word. She wondered if the poor man could sense the animosity in the air between his customers.

Fatigue hit her like a brick dropped from a great height. She was tired of struggling, of making ends meet, of paddling her own canoe and getting nowhere. Why not marry a rich man and be done with the effort?

She gasped at the cynical thought. Her expectations of life might have changed, but her views on marriage hadn't.

Her gaze went to Caleb, drawn to him against her will. He had once been her fiancé…her love…her lover.

Heat swept through her. She'd given herself and her love in the first flames of rapture without a thought of tomorrow. She would be much more cautious in the future.

"So you're a teacher," Caleb drawled. His lips curled into an attractive smile. It was also sardonic. "Is this a new kick?"

"It's how I make my living," she said stiffly. "And have been for the past five years, as noted in my résumé."

One thick dark eyebrow lifted slightly. When she'd first met him, she'd been fascinated by that expressive gesture. Coupled with the smile that hovered at the corners of his mouth, it seemed to mock the world, to dare it to thwart him. She'd wanted to be like that—bold and insouciant.

She had let herself care too much, she thought, knowing it was one of her major faults. Other people's misfortunes touched her heart. But no more. She was tougher now.

He retrieved the letter and read over her qualifications. He looked up, his eyebrow raised slightly. "Impressive. So you found your calling, huh?"

She felt the sting of his mockery. "I like teaching, yes."

"Having done that all year, why aren't you spending the summer on the Riviera like your friend Sue?"

Eden studied his expression, trying to figure him out. At the genuine question in his eyes, she realized he was puzzled by her application for the job of tutoring his son. It came to her that he knew nothing of her life since their stormy parting.

Sue had kept her informed of his life, but he hadn't been interested enough to inquire about hers. Her love for him had been part of her life; his feelings for her had been but a passing fancy, not very important in the grand scheme of things.

"I have to work for a living, Caleb. So does my mother."

He didn't quite believe her. "What happened to your father?"

"He died the summer after our…after you and I…after my sophomore year in college. A heart attack. At his office. While Mother and I waited and waited all weekend for him to join us at the beach house. The security guard found him at two o'clock Sunday morning, slumped over a stock report."

"I'm sorry."

She looked into his eyes and saw a flicker of sympathy. She nodded and looked away.

"Sue didn't tell me," he began, then paused, frowning.

"Did you ever ask?"

"No," he said bluntly. "You were a part of my life I wanted to forget…quickly and completely."

"You succeeded," she said, speaking the truth aloud. It still hurt. Some things never got better with time, it seemed. "You married six months later and had a son the year after that." She felt the sting of tears again, but she said the words. "I'm sorry about your wife."

She didn't want to look at him, but she couldn't help it. She saw the regret, the intense sorrow, that appeared for a second in his dark eyes, before his expression hardened.

"She was a kind and lovely person," he said. "She deserved more from life."

So he had loved his wife.

Eden thought she had long ago faced the fact that he hadn't truly loved her but she hadn't envisioned this meeting and his cool indifference to her presence. She tried to think of something to say, but failed.

A line from a poem came to her, "Too deep for tears." Some things were like that.

"Well, I've taken up enough of your time." She laid her napkin on the table and picked up her purse.

He stood when she did. She managed a smile, but she didn't offer to shake hands. "Goodbye, Caleb," she said; then she walked away without looking back.

After stopping by a couple of employment agencies, Eden returned home to an empty house. Her mom was at the museum where she worked as a secretary during the day and did docent tours in the evening to supplement their income.

A note on the refrigerator told her to call Sue. Eden ignored the message. She spent the rest of the afternoon and evening lost in memories of being swept off her feet by the most exciting man she'd ever met.

Sue had been the connection. She was a second cousin to Caleb and had invited him to her Christmas party that long-ago winter. Eden had been invited, too.

She and Sue had met at college that year. They'd been assigned the same room in the dorm and had become fast friends.

To Sue's surprise, Caleb had shown up at Christmas. Late, of course. If Eden had been wiser, she might had taken that as a clue to the future. But she hadn't been wise. She'd been in love.

Their eyes had met when he walked in the door. He'd come straight over to her and, without taking his eyes off her, had demanded an introduction from his cousin. Sue had laughed and warned Eden not to get mixed up with her handsome cousin.

"He must have a girl in every port," she'd said, "the way he zooms around the world."

"No such luck," he'd replied in his deep, seductive voice, which had later whispered other things in Eden's trusting ears. "Coffee, sugar, tea, spices. Those keep me on the road and occupied."

No warning had penetrated Eden's happy haze, not even

when she and Sue had discussed Caleb at three in the morning, sitting on Sue's bed and rehashing the party.

"He's a workaholic," Sue had said with a grimace. "His father is the same…or was, until he had a stroke. Involvement with a man like that makes a lonely life for a woman."

Eden had found out how lonely during the next five months. Caleb had missed their dates more and more often as he took care of the press of business all over the world. She lost track of where he was.

Nearly missing their engagement party in May had been the last straw. She wouldn't live the life her mother did.

Eden's father had been like a guest who came and went without warning. He'd missed all the main events of her life. But he'd been there for the engagement party—she had made him promise. She hadn't thought to extract the same promise from her fiancé, though.

Hugging her arms around her knees, Eden sat on the window seat in her bedroom, in the Victorian house that had been her home for twenty-six years. It took all her and her mother's resources to keep the place up.

Caleb's family home was a brick mansion set on lush acreage well out of the city, although an expensive suburb now encroached on one side of their property. A private country club, complete with a lake for boating, was on the other side.

It wasn't until she'd met Sue and Caleb that she'd realized her father, a lawyer, had been merely well-off, not rich. His income had stopped when he died. The investments he'd made, even those with Eden's inheritance from her maternal grandparents, had been ill-advised.

There had been enough money to pay off the mortgage and get Eden through college—her mother had insisted on that—but they'd both had to work. Eden and Sue had remained best friends, thus Eden had known of Caleb's marriage and the birth of the child.

The unkindest cut of all, she thought, mocking her foolish heart. The knowledge that the man whose children she had wanted to have had married another and sired a child had signified the final chapter of one phase of her life.

That was a long time ago, she reminded herself. So many of her hopes and dreams had been bundled up and set aside during those first two years of college.

A true learning experience, those two years, she acknowledged. Caleb's son had been born a month after Eden's father died. She'd learned that a birth could be as painful to the heart as a death.

The clock chimed, reminding her it was time for her mother to arrive home. She went downstairs and prepared a snack.

"How did the interview go?" Jane Sommers asked over a glass of ice tea, after they'd chatted awhile about the museum. She eyed the last cookie left on the plate, sighed, then ignored it.

"I didn't get the job." Eden shrugged and smiled. "Remember when you used to tell me that if something seemed too good to be true, it usually was? So was this job."

"Too many applicants?"

"Well, no. The wrong employer."

Jane raised her brows.

"Caleb Remmick," Eden explained. "He has a son. Did I ever mention that to you?"

"No, you never did," Jane said slowly.

Eden saw the compassion in her mother's eyes and looked away. "He does. The boy is five. He'll be six in August. I guess his mother was French—"

"Was?"

"She died. Of a fever, Sue said. Some kind of lung infection that antibiotics couldn't cure. Caleb and his family had a house on a Caribbean island—Martinique. Now he wants to bring his son back to the States to start school. Josh—his name is Joshua—needs some brushing up in English."

"The poor child. Can you imagine the adjustment he'll have to go through—a new home, a new school and new friends, on top of his mother's death?"

Eden thought of her father's death, of how strange the world had seemed without him in it, even though she'd rarely seen him. The loss of a parent severed a link that couldn't be replaced.

Her heart went out to the boy. If he saw as little of Caleb as she'd seen of her own father, then the move would seem like going to a foreign land and living with strangers.

"I'll speak to Sue," Eden decided.

"Her daughter is only four," Jane pointed out.

"Yes, but she knows other people with kids."

"Isn't she leaving for France in a week, to spend the summer?"

Eden frowned. "Yes. She's probably going insane with the packing and all. She won't have time for Josh until they return in September. By then it'll be too late."

"Well, I suppose there's nothing we can do." Her mother peered again at the remaining cookie. She picked it up and took a bite. "I'll walk an extra hour tomorrow," she said.

Eden put their dishes in the dishwasher and wiped off the table. "Tomorrow we fix the porch, remember?"

"That's my day off," Jane grumbled. "However, I suppose we'd better. The postman nearly fell through a step this morning."

"Did we get any interesting mail?"

"We get another chance to win ten million dollars from that magazine company," Jane said with a droll grin.

"Well, we'd better get the porch fixed before the prize patrol shows up to tell us about it. We don't want them falling through the planks and getting knocked out before we get the award."

"Right. With our luck, they'd sue and get all the money."

"Mom, I've got to talk to you about this cynical attitude of yours," Eden advised, following her mother out of the big, old-fashioned kitchen.

One thing had come out of those hard times, Eden thought, slipping into a cotton nightgown a few minutes later. She and her mother had gotten to be friends.

As she crawled into bed, a wayward thought came to her. Once she'd thought of sharing late-night confidences with Caleb, then going to sleep in his arms. After making love.

A restless yearning came over her. Heat radiated from the secret part of her body that only Caleb had found.

She pushed the memories away and tried to count sheep. She shouldn't have listened to Sue…. Sue! Her friend—her *best* friend…had to have known the job entailed working for Caleb. That explained the urging to rush down there right away without calling first…before any other applicants could even inquire about the position.

Eden realized the whole interview had been an elaborate setup, one that Sue couldn't have perpetrated alone. Her friend couldn't plan her way out of a paper bag.

So who had been behind the scheme?

Her heart beat faster as possibilities raced through her mind.

Chapter Two

The streets were familiar to Caleb as he wound his way through the neighborhood of stately homes— mostly old Victorians, a few Tudors, here and there a new structure. He could almost drive it blindfolded... even after seven years.

He could recall dashing from the airport to this house, eager to see his love. *Love*. Ha! Eden had loved him as long as he did exactly what she wanted. She gave no credence to the press of work and the things a man had to do to make it in today's world.

Briefly, he wondered what the hell he was doing there.

Even as he thought it, he turned into the drive covered with river pebbles. It curved in front of the graceful white Victorian home, flanked by a riot of summer flowers. He stopped the motor and stepped out of the car.

The front porch wrapped around one side of the house. Where the porch turned the corner, it swept out into a circle covered by a rounded roof, forming an attached gazebo. A swing was mounted from the rafters of the gazebo on sturdy chains.

Eden, her back to him, was guiding an electric saw along a board. The saw's high whine had drowned out the noise of his tires on the gravel drive.

His breath stopped, literally stopped, while he stared at her.

She was on her knees, her back to him, dressed in cutoff jeans that were ragged around the edges. Little strings brushed seductively along the backs of her thighs.

Hunger, so sharp it was painful, ripped through him.

He wanted to grab her and yank her into his car, where, sitting in the driveway during that cold spring, they'd shared kisses so passionate the flames had burned right through his control. One night he couldn't take it any longer.

"Come with me," he'd said hoarsely.

She hadn't even asked where.

He'd taken her to his office in the Remmick Building. There, in the heart of Chicago, with the lights of other sky-scrapers blinking at them through the windows, they'd made love on the carpet while a light snow fell on the city.

The pang of sensual hunger bit deeper. He cursed aloud just as the saw stopped. Eden whipped around, staring over her shoulder at him, still on her hands and knees. She leaped to her feet like a startled gazelle.

One part of him noted she was still as graceful as ever, her body almost coltish in its slenderness. She was still beautiful. He frowned at his stupidity in coming here.

Eden saw Caleb's mouth harden into a thin line of disapproval. She became acutely aware of her old, ragged outfit. Caleb was dressed in expensive slacks and a white shirt, the sleeves rolled up a couple of turns above his wrists.

The playful breeze tousled his coal black hair, which was unruly enough without the added disarray. The sun sparkled off each wind-tossed wave. She wanted to comb her fingers through the thick strands....

Taking a deep breath, she put the saw down and pushed the safety goggles up on top of her head. "Caleb," she said. "This is a surprise." She sounded as if she were speaking to a neighbor she hadn't seen in some time instead of to the man she'd once thought was the love of her life.

He smiled, not in amusement and certainly not as if he were glad to see her, and came up the porch steps. "Yes, I suppose it is," he agreed.

His voice was a melody, warm and delightful, like the promise of spring after a long, cold winter. A shimmer of emotion slid down her spine. Regret, longing, anger—she wasn't sure which.

"Be careful," she said. "The porch is a hazard."

She tried not to notice how attractive he was. He sported a tan and glowed with the essence of life. She felt like a drudge by comparison—the little match girl meets Prince Charming.

"So I see." He took a seat in the swing and surveyed her work. "Is this a new hobby?"

She grimaced ruefully. "Hardly. It comes under the heading of repairs. Keeping the floor under one's feet, so to speak."

And keeping one's feet on the floor, she advised herself. When she looked at him, she felt lighter than air, like dandelion fluff blowing in the wind, her thoughts tending to scatter in all directions. She wanted to look at him, just look and look...

It wasn't fair to still feel this way after so many years, she protested inwardly. She was nervous and unstrung, while he sat and calmly watched her, his gaze dark and unreadable.

Caleb was the ultimate tycoon, she reminded herself.

The effect of his expensive clothes and tasseled loafers was casual, but everything about him whispered of wealth and the ruthlessness that went with it.

"So what brings you out here?" she asked brightly.

"You."

A ripple of unease danced along her nerves. "Blunt and to the point, as always," she noted.

"I've never seen any reason to be different."

"No, I suppose you wouldn't." She smiled, and felt her lips tremble ever so slightly.

His gaze narrowed on that telltale sign, but he said nothing. Darn him for his inscrutable ways.

"What do you want, Caleb?" she asked, not bothering to soften the sharpness in her tone. "I have a lot of work to do today."

"I talked to Sue."

Eden searched his face for some clue to the conversation. She regretted that she hadn't called her friend back.

"So?" she said, as if she hadn't the slightest interest.

He sighed and leaned forward in the swing, resting his arms on his thighs and staring at the new boards she'd nailed into place that morning.

"She told me of your…circumstances."

Blood beat its way up into her face. "My finances, you mean?" She shrugged in a carelessly defiant manner. She wasn't going to try to hide her lack of money, but neither was she going to discuss it with him.

He frowned and looked up at her. The morning light hit his eyes as he shifted. For a second, they seemed to blaze at her with a barely controlled anger.

She instinctively recoiled; then he settled back in the swing and the fury was gone. He watched her, without any emotion that she could detect. She gave him an insouciant smile.

"Your finances…among other things," he admitted.

"What things?" she snapped.

"Your father." He paused.

Eden didn't respond.

Caleb sighed. "You're as difficult to talk to now as you were seven years ago."

Her heart contracted into a painful knot at the mention of their previous time together. It wasn't fair that it should still hurt, not after all this time!

She wondered if he remembered telling her not to be a fool when she'd broken off with him. She'd replied she'd been a fool to fall in love with someone like him. She still felt that way.

"True," she agreed. "So why did you bother to come?"

"To tell you the job is yours."

Her mouth fell open.

"As Taft noted, your qualifications are excellent. And no one else seems to want the job." His smile was self-mocking.

Footsteps in the house saved her from answering. Her mother came out. "I thought I heard voices... Oh!"

Caleb stood. He stepped over the lumber and the cord to the saw and held out his hand. "Hello, Jane." His smile was genuine. "As lovely as ever," he remarked.

Eden grimaced. Her mother was dressed in jeans and a neat cotton blouse, ready to help with the work. She had also put on makeup and earrings. Eden hadn't bothered.

"Caleb, I'm so glad to see you." Jane put her hand in his.

Instead of shaking it, he brought it to his lips and lightly kissed the back in a gesture so warm and natural it set Eden's teeth on edge. She watched her mother succumb to Caleb's charm.

He's the enemy, Eden wanted to shout.

He and her mother had always gotten along. There had

been affection and respect between them from the first, independent of Eden and his involvement and problems.

When Caleb swung his gaze back to her, it was hard and cold. She retreated a step. "Would you like some coffee?" she heard herself ask.

"That would be lovely," Jane said before he could refuse. "And bring some of those cookies you made." She smiled at Caleb. "Eden has been baking up a storm since school let out. I think she's bored."

"I've offered her a job," he said.

"Why, that's wonderful." Jane beamed at Eden. "Isn't that wonderful, darling? This solves all your problems."

Eden clamped her mouth shut before she said something she'd regret. She whirled and went into the house.

Emotions boiled through her as she slapped mugs onto a tray and filled them with coffee. He couldn't just appear in her life and take over, she fumed. Work for him? That'd be the day. She'd rather starve. Which was what she'd been going to say before her mother had interrupted.

But there was the summer to get through, her conscience nagged at her.

So she'd get a job at a fast-food place.

She placed napkins, a plate of cookies, cream and sugar on the tray along with a spoon. Only her mother took cream and sugar.

Walking up the hall, she heard Caleb and her mother conversing like old friends long parted and now joyously reunited. She set her lips firmly together. It made no difference to her.

Balancing the tray on one hand, she opened the front door and stepped out. Leaving the door ajar, she let the screened storm door slam behind her. Taking the tray in both hands again, she noted the gabbing had stopped the minute she reappeared.

Caleb sprang up and took the tray. He held it for Jane while she prepared her cup of coffee and selected a cookie. Then he held it out to Eden, who'd taken a seat at the edge of the porch, her back against a support column, one leg dangling over the boxwood hedge she'd clipped the day before.

She saw his gaze sweep over her and pause on her bare thigh. His chest lifted in a quick breath, and she knew, as if she were in his mind, exactly what he was thinking.

Heat shattered her composure as she remembered his hands on her, stroking along her legs, his voice telling her how he loved the feel of her—so smooth, so warm...all woman...his woman.

Eden grabbed a mug. "I don't take anything in mine," she said, her voice as cold as she could make it.

His eyes met hers. "Since when?" he asked softly.

Then he dared to smile at her, the knowledge of her awareness of his thoughts in his look. He cocked his head to the side, a challenge in the gesture.

Sharing coffee after sharing passion had become a habit. He'd had a coffeemaker in his office, but never cream or sugar. She'd learned to drink it without, the way he did. After the breakup, she hadn't bothered reverting to her old ways.

He set the tray on the two sawhorses, picked up his mug and returned to the swing beside her mother. "I'm impressed with the job you're doing here," he said. "Perhaps while you're coaching Josh in English you could also teach him carpentry."

Eden gave him a furious glance. "I'm not going to teach your son anything."

"Caleb was teasing," Jane said gently to Eden.

"You don't have to explain Caleb to me, Mother. I know him quite well." She wished she could have bitten off the words before they'd spilled out, but it was too late. "I'm sorry," she added at once. "I didn't mean to snap."

"I understand," her mother replied, sympathy in her smile. She turned to Caleb. "I wish *I* could take the job. However, I have a full schedule this summer. It's our busiest time. Tell me about the child. Where is he now?"

"In Martinique with his grandparents. He'll arrive in the States this coming Sunday. I'd hoped to have someone hired and ready to meet him—"

"Meet him?" Eden broke in. "You'd have a stranger meet him?" Another thought occurred to her. "Who's flying with him?"

"He's coming solo."

"Solo!" Eden echoed in horror. "A five-year-old child?"

Caleb gave her a hard look. "Josh is very excited about it. He's flown several times between the island and Chicago."

"Alone?" she demanded.

"Of course not. This is his first trip alone."

"And you were going to hire a tutor this week and have her meet the plane on Sunday?"

"Yes." His tone dared her to make something of it.

"He must be quite mature for his age," Jane hurriedly put in.

Caleb nodded. "He is."

"Where will you be while this five-year-old flies several thousand miles *solo?*" Eden spoke very quietly.

Caleb held her gaze. "I have meetings in Washington, D.C., part of this week and all of next."

Eden threw her coffee out into the grass in lieu of throwing it at Caleb. She stood and placed the mug on the tray before she faced him. "I always knew you were a heartless bastard, Caleb. I just never knew how heartless until now."

"Eden!" Jane exclaimed.

Eden walked off, her hands clenched at her sides. She went into the house, up to her room and locked the door.

When she sat on the cushion of the window seat and drew her knees up to her chest, she realized she was shaking with anger.

A child. And Caleb thought no more of the boy than he had of her years ago. Nothing mattered but *his* schedule, *his* work, *his* plans. Nothing and no one. How could she have ever thought to make a difference in his life?

She heard footsteps in the hall and knew whose they were. She stared at the door while Caleb tried the knob, found it locked, then banged on the wooden panel.

"Eden, I want to talk to you," he said.

Recognizing the determination, she went over, unsnapped the lock and threw open the door. He walked into her bedroom, a place he'd never been the whole time they'd been engaged.

He thrust his hands into his pockets. Red flags of anger blazed in his cheeks. She returned to the window seat and watched him without speaking.

Caleb throttled an impulse to sweep her up, lay her on the bed and kiss her until she melted under him.

She continued to stare at him, her eyes hot and dry, filled with loathing.

The guilt he'd been fighting all week washed over him. His life suddenly seemed a mess—too complicated, too rushed, too…everything. And his son was the one who suffered for it.

Taking a calming breath, he paced the room. "My schedule got messed up. The Senate hearings on import tariffs were moved ahead by two weeks—"

"You're meeting on the weekend, too?" she inquired, her brows arching upward in disbelief.

"No, but we have meetings clear through Saturday afternoon, and we start again on Monday."

"Huh!" she said, as if that concluded her argument.

"Dammit," he began. He paced to the mirrored closet doors and back to the window. He stopped in front of her.

The sun backlighted her until she seemed to glow. She stared at him with her light, sherry-colored eyes, her attitude condemning and without mercy. As usual. Nothing had changed between them.

Why the hell was he trying to explain anything to her? She had nothing to do with his life. She'd opted out seven years ago in this very house, throwing a glass of champagne at him, then heading out the door into the garden, leaving him standing there in a crowd of gaping faces, some embarrassed, some gleeful.

He suddenly remembered how she'd looked when he'd walked out of the gaily decorated room and found her.

She'd been sitting on a bench among the roses, the moonlight pouring over her like molten silver, her white evening dress shimmering as she drew her knees up and wrapped her arms around them. She had seemed like a lovely goddess, distant, cold and disdainful of humans.

He had wanted to take her in his arms and crush her to him, to tell her how sorry he was. He'd wanted to grovel at her feet and beg for another chance. Then she'd spoken to him in a tone he'd never before heard from her.

"I never want to see you again," she'd said.

He'd turned and walked away, shocked by the loathing in her voice, chilled by the fact that she wouldn't look at him.

"To hell with it!" he said now. He walked out of her bedroom, ran down the carpeted stairs and outside.

"Caleb," Jane said, worry in her face.

He stopped, took control of his churning anger and managed a smile. "I don't think she wants the job," he said lightly.

Her smile was sad. "I suppose not." She patted his arm.

"But it was…kind of you to think of offering it. I'd hoped—"

"I didn't offer it," he said, to put the record straight. Another wave of anger hit him. "I was set up—"

"Not by Eden," Jane stated. "She'd never do that. She's too honest to try something underhanded."

Caleb hadn't been thinking of Eden. However, he wasn't sure Jane was right. Women seemed devious creatures to him, each with her own agenda. "I didn't mean Eden," he agreed, "but I think I know who might have been in on this little farce—mainly my father and dear Cousin Sue."

The anger surged anew in him. Damn them for interfering in his life. He'd nip this in the bud—

"I'm sure they were only thinking of your welfare," Jane said, in her usual kind manner.

"My welfare is my concern."

"What about the welfare of your son?" she asked.

He heard the undertone of disapproval. Dammit, everyone was ganging up on him. His father wanted him to establish a *real* home for the boy. Sue thought he should provide a mother for Josh. Eden had made him sound like a callous jerk for hiring someone to help Josh make the transition from Martinique to Chicago. Now Jane, the one person he'd thought was on his side, was hinting that he wasn't thinking of Josh at all.

If he did marry again, it sure as hell wouldn't be to Eden. The pain of her rejection seven years ago ground into him. He swore inwardly once again. One would think a person would get over that after all the time that had passed.

"My son understands how things are," he growled. "He knows a man has things to do, even if he doesn't like doing them."

Jane stepped away from him. "Perhaps Eden was right," she said slowly. "Perhaps you haven't a heart after all." She looked disappointed in him.

"Perhaps," he agreed. "Or maybe I'm too smart to wear it on my sleeve the way I did with your daughter."

He regretted the remark as soon as he made it. Jane merely nodded noncommittally. A lady all the way, he thought, but a picture of her daughter slipped into his mind.

"I have to go," he said on a softer note. "Thanks for your hospitality, Jane. You've always been…kind."

She suddenly smiled. "Give Eden a couple of days to stew. I think she'll come around."

He hesitated, then nodded. Grimly, he marched out to the car and drove off without a backward glance at the upstairs window.

Eden parked her eight-year-old car, her high school graduation gift from her parents, in the country club lot. It looked out of place next to the sporty models and expensive sedans.

Today was Wednesday, the day she and Sue always met for lunch, if possible. She had a few questions to ask her best friend.

She hurried across the pavement, through the building and into the restaurant. Sue was already at the table. Eden joined her.

"You don't look any the worse for wear," Sue commented, giving her a droll grin.

Eden accepted a menu from the waiter and sat down opposite her friend. "Who else was in on the conspiracy?" she asked.

Sue tried to look innocent.

Eden had to smile. "Drop the picture-of-injured-innocence act. I know you too well."

"You aren't mad?" Sue hedged.

"I'm not sure," Eden admitted. "Did…did Caleb tell you to send me over there for that interview?"

"Uh, why would you think that?" Sue peered at her, then hid behind the large, elaborate menu.

"Because there were no other applicants?" Eden suggested, letting sarcasm creep into her tone. "Because the firm was one of the most expensive headhunter outfits in the country? Because it was located in the Remmick Building?"

"Ah, there really is a Mary Poppins," Sue drawled. She had the nerve to give Eden a big grin, no longer trying to deny her part in the plot.

"Right. Who was your helper, besides Mary Poppins?"

Her friend held up both hands in surrender. "It was Caleb's father."

Eden was totally surprised. Immediately after that, she felt a slight letdown. So it hadn't been Caleb. She hadn't really thought he would seek her out.

"He called me a month ago," Sue explained, "and told me of Caleb's plans to bring Josh back here. He wanted me to help the child make some friends before school started, but I'd already planned to go to France with Gerard."

Sue's husband represented several restaurants and traveled widely to select wines for them. He took his wife and child with him on his travels as much as possible, Eden knew. Sue was lucky. Her husband hated to be without his family.

"I suggested they put Josh in one of the summer programs here at the club," Sue continued, "but he wasn't sure about that. He said Caleb wanted Josh to have some tutoring in English."

"I see," Eden murmured dryly.

"Yes. I saw the light, one might say. You'd just had word that your summer job was cancelled. Voilà, the perfect solution. Caleb's dad liked it, too," Sue added modestly.

"So you two planned it, and Caleb and I were suckered in."

"Oh-oh," Sue said sotto voce. "Don't look now—"

Eden turned toward the entrance. Her heart lurched. Caleb stood there. "Did you plan this, too?" she demanded.

"No. But let's ask him to join us." Sue started to rise and motion to Caleb.

"Don't!" Eden whispered fiercely. She didn't want to talk to him, not after their contretemps yesterday.

Her friend looked puzzled. "Why not? You're going to be working for him—"

"I refused the job."

Sue stared at her blankly, then frowned. "Eden, this is carrying pride too far," she began. She stopped as her gaze swept back to the front of the restaurant. "Damn," she exclaimed softly, looking disappointed.

Eden glanced over her shoulder once more. A beautiful redhead now stood beside Caleb, hanging on his arm and smiling up at him. She looked about twenty-two.

Without betraying any emotion, Eden turned back to the table. "The latest debutante?" she inquired with a sardonic air.

Sue shrugged. "He sees us." She glanced around. "There aren't any tables free. I'm going to invite them over."

Without so much as a "by your leave," she stood up and motioned to Caleb. "They're coming this way," she announced triumphantly as she sat down again.

Eden gave her a fulminating glance, then pasted a smile on her face. Caleb loomed beside her, looking much more than six feet tall. He seated his companion in one of the empty chairs and took the one opposite.

"Nice of you to have us," he said conversationally. "I forgot to call for a reservation." He introduced the redhead. "Mona's firm is handling an ad campaign for our gourmet coffee division. We're selling direct to the consumer through an ordering service."

"That's something new, isn't it?" Sue asked.

He nodded.

"We're very excited about it," Mona said in a slightly breathless voice. "We'll be advertising in all the women's magazines." She named several prominent magazines that would appeal to higher-income-bracket families.

"Are you the secretary?" Eden blurted, unable to hold in her curiosity about Mona's place in the scheme of things.

"Oh, no," she murmured, as if shocked at the idea. "I'm in charge of ad liaison with the magazines. I'll be working very closely with Caleb on the campaign."

Eden realized she'd been put in her place but good. "How very interesting," she said, making her voice sound as sincere as possible.

"Yes, it is," Mona said with a superior smile. "My father owns the firm, so I get the plums." She smiled at Caleb, as if about to take a bite out of him.

"Oh," Eden said, and was unable to think of another thing to add to that.

Sue hid a grin behind her water glass.

"Mona is very good at her job," Caleb assured them.

"What do you two do?" Mona asked.

"I teach school," Eden said, feeling more than a little outclassed.

"I'm my husband's chief advisor," Sue declared. "He doesn't dare make a move without consulting me."

"I'll vouch for that," Caleb put in. To Eden's surprise, he laughed in genuine amusement and raised his water glass in a toast to his cousin.

If she and Caleb had married, they would have been friends with Sue and Gerard, Eden thought with nostalgic longing. As couples, they would have gone to plays and concerts. Their children would have been friends. If they had married…

No, that was useless speculation. Life was what it was and wishing didn't change it. These chance meetings with Caleb would soon end. With Sue gone, Eden wouldn't be returning to the club, since she and her mother no longer belonged.

Her gaze was drawn to the lovely redhead. *She* obviously belonged in Caleb's world. Eden listened as Sue asked Mona about advertising, wondering if it was worth the cost. They started discussing the issue.

"Have you found a job for the summer yet?" Caleb asked Eden.

She shook her head. "The employment agency called this morning. They may have something next week."

He drummed his fingers on the table impatiently. "My father came up with a plan. Since it's hard for him to get around these days, his valet will meet Josh and pick up his luggage."

So Caleb had found a way out of his dilemma.

"Henry is almost as old as my father." Caleb drummed his fingers again, then cursed under his breath. He gave Eden a direct look, one of appeal, she realized.

"I'd feel better having someone I trusted with kids meet him," he said. "Someone who is young and used to children. Someone who would take him to museums and movies. My son needs a friend." The admission seemed hard for him to make.

A knot formed in Eden's throat as she pictured the child. A boy…a lonely little boy. "That's not fair," she said, pity for the child choking her.

"I know."

"There must be plenty of people available."

"Yes." Caleb leaned so close, his breath stirred the hair over her ear. "My father wants you. He says I'm to grovel if I have to. Shall I?"

She stared at him, spellbound by this side of him she'd never seen. "Would you?" The words were out before she could stop them, and she felt a blush sweep up her neck.

Caleb smoothed down a wisp of her sun-streaked hair. Would he beg? He hadn't when she'd walked out on him. He'd thought she would be the one to crawl back when she realized what a good catch she was giving up.

He recognized with a start that he was angry that she seemed to be happy in her life without him, that she had made it on her own with no help from him during her troubles.

When Sue had told him about Eden's father, he'd felt a stir of triumph. Eden could have had all the money she could spend if she'd been reasonable. Neither she nor her mother would've had to work when Mr. Sommers had died and left them with a pile of debt and bad investments.

If she'd married him, he would have given her everything in the world, everything that was his to give, everything....

He stopped that line of thought. She'd had her chance. Eden had trampled on his heart and his pride. The only position he was offering her now was that of tutor to his son.

"Take it or leave it," he said.

Chapter Three

"I'll take it," Eden said.

"Take what?" Mona asked, turning from Sue's determined questions to the conversation between the other two.

Eden waited for Caleb to answer. She couldn't believe she'd said she'd take the job. It had been a moment of madness.

A moment of weakness, she forced herself to admit. She'd always been weak where Caleb was concerned, unable to deny him anything. Perhaps he'd refuse to accept her in the position now that he'd gotten his way in the matter.

"The job of tutoring my son," Caleb answered, his eyes never leaving Eden's.

He didn't look pleased, she noted. Maybe cornered was the correct term. Sue and his father had counted on Caleb's need to find someone on short notice. They'd had over a month to hire a tutor, but had let it go until the last week.

"What time does his plane get in?" she asked. She knew when she'd been outmaneuvered.

"Noon on Sunday." He named the airline and gave her the flight number.

"I'll be there," Eden promised, thinking of a frightened child alighting in a barely remembered city with only strangers to greet him. "If your father is well enough, I'd like for him to accompany me. The boy will have enough stress without coping with a total stranger when he arrives. You'd better give me his full name. The flight attendant will probably ask."

Caleb nodded. "His name is Josh," he said. "Joshua Caleb Remmick."

His gaze locked with hers. Eden couldn't look away. They had once considered children's names together. That was one thing they'd both agreed on: they'd wanted children right away.

"That's lovely, Caleb," the redhead interrupted. "Is Joshua an old family name?"

"No. My wife wanted a biblical name to go with mine."

Sue and Mona launched into a discussion of baby names. Mona thought she wanted three children, but she wasn't sure. "That would depend on the father," she graciously conceded, with a smiling glance at Caleb.

By the time Caleb and his companion left them, Eden had a fierce headache. She tried to calm the uneasiness in her heart. Caleb still had a pull on her that was worrisome. She recognized danger when it stared her in the face.

"Well," Sue said, beaming at her. She lifted her eyebrows in open triumph.

"No one likes people who gloat," Eden informed her friend.

"Did I say a word?"

"No, but you're smiling like a mouse in a cheese shop."

While Sue laughed, Eden laid her napkin aside and prepared to leave. There was still the porch to finish. She'd do it today…in case she won the ten-million-dollar prize. *Dream on.*

She recalled that a recent article in the business section of the Sunday paper had listed Caleb and his father in the top ten percent of the richest people in Chicago.

She bet they had never had to get on their hands and knees and nail in new boards on their porch. Caleb should try it. That kind of work was probably good for the soul. At any rate, it gave a person lots of time to think.

In all fairness, Caleb had never seemed rich to her. He'd been at ease in her home, which, while nice, wasn't a mansion. He was a regular person, with no airs that she'd ever noticed.

Right. He was wonderful, she thought, mocking her memories. Except that he'd put everything else first, before her and their love. That hadn't been so wonderful, she'd soon discovered.

She drove home, changed clothes and resumed her chores. She finished as twilight was turning the sky interesting shades of lavender and dusky blue. Tomorrow she'd start painting, she decided, pressing her hands into the small of her back.

A car turned into the drive. She watched Caleb park and climb out. He'd removed his suit coat and tie and had rolled his sleeves up the way they'd been yesterday when he'd come to the house. She, of course, was in her oldest shorts and T-shirt, with a pair of worn sneakers on her feet and sawdust in her hair.

He came up the steps and looked around. "Good job."

"Thanks." She wound the cord around the saw and put it in a plastic dishpan for storage on a garage shelf. "I assume you're here to discuss my duties before you leave?"

"Yes."

"Will it take long? I want to put this stuff away and sweep the porch before it gets completely dark."

Caleb frowned. "Have you been working all day on this?"

"I stopped for lunch," she reminded him.

"But not for dinner. Is Jane working tonight?"

"Yes." Eden gave him a wary look.

"I'll get a pizza while you finish up," he volunteered. So saying, he took off, leaving her standing there gazing after him and wondering if he was as concerned as he'd sounded.

Giving herself a mental shake at the ridiculous thought, she bent to the task of tidying up. After putting her tools away and sweeping up, she replaced the furniture in the porch gazebo where the swing was.

Caleb wasn't back. She dashed upstairs and took a quick shower. After running a comb through her hair, she let it air dry while she dressed in clean slacks and a cotton sweater. Wearing white sandals, she went back to the porch.

Caleb was sitting on the swing, waiting.

She walked over, feeling self-conscious all at once. A pizza box was on the table between the two Adirondack chairs. Two soft drinks were next to it.

"Dinner," Caleb said, his voice quiet and somehow reserved.

They had shared meals like this in the past. "Smells good," she said.

She chose one of the white wooden chairs with blue-and-gold-striped chintz pillows. Caleb moved to the other chair, which had red-and-gold pillows. He opened the box.

"Oh, I'll get plates," she said.

"I had them put in some paper ones." He lifted a bag and retrieved paper plates and napkins. After loading one plate with a huge slice of pizza, he handed it to her along with a napkin, then fixed his own.

Eden ate and watched the twilight descend. The trees formed a black silhouette against the brighter western sky. Several stars were visible. Nostalgia gripped her heart.

One summer, she'd looked at the stars and had seen every dream she'd dared dream coming true…a husband she adored, a home, their children. One summer long ago…

"I assume you aren't packed yet," Caleb stated, polishing off one piece of pizza and reaching for another.

"Packed?" she repeated. The word made no sense.

He set his plate on the table, wiped his fingers and took a long drink of cola. "I'd like you to get moved in and settled before you go to pick up Josh."

"Moved?" She realized she sounded as if she'd never heard the word before, but in truth, she couldn't figure out what he meant.

"To the house. To *my* house," he said when she looked blank.

She was astounded. "Why would I move to your house? I have a perfectly good house of my own. Which I intend to paint before school starts in September."

He gave her an impatient stare and shook his head. "That wasn't the deal. You were to live at the house—"

"No one said anything about living at your house. I'm a teacher, not a nanny."

Caleb glowered at her. "Taft didn't tell you?"

"No."

"I suppose Sue didn't mention it, either."

"No."

He drew a breath that was redolent of controlled irritation. "Well, that's part of the job."

She raised her chin. "Not as far as I'm concerned."

"Dammit, Eden," Caleb snapped at her. He stopped and sought composure, then started again. "Don't you think I know this will be a hard adjustment for my son? I want someone he can trust to be there twenty-four hours a day while he's settling in. Why do you think the job pays three times more than the going rate?"

"I hadn't thought about it," she admitted, her mind in a whirl. "I agree it would be better to have someone with him that he can depend on…since it's obvious you're never there for him."

She immediately regretted the gibe as being underhanded and below the belt. It wasn't her place to tell Caleb how to raise his son. But she did feel sorry for the child.

A brick-red flush spread up Caleb's neck and into his face. "Don't push me too far," he warned. "I'm tired. I'm worried about Josh, no matter what you may think, and I'm in no mood for a lesson on parenthood by—" He stopped abruptly.

"Go ahead," she challenged. "Let's hear the rest of it."

"By a woman who walked out on her own engagement party." His voice was as hard as a ten-penny nail.

"Because her fiancé didn't care enough to be on time," she reminded him, her tone just as hard.

Caleb bit angrily into another slice of pizza. They ate in silence for a minute. "Josh could have been our son," he said, his voice so low and tense she wasn't sure she'd heard him right.

She met his gaze. The streetlight suddenly blinked on and shone in his eyes, but she couldn't read his thoughts in those dark, accusing depths.

"What if he were our child?" he continued in a muted tone.

"If he were mine…" She stopped as unexpected emotion formed a ball in her throat. She laid the plate on the table and leaped to her feet, horrified as tears welled in her eyes.

When she and Caleb had broken their engagement, she'd vowed never to cry over a man again. To cry over the same one was foolish in the extreme. To let him *make* her cry was plain stupid.

He blocked her escape from the gazebo. His hands settled on her shoulders and wouldn't let go when she tried to squirm away from his touch.

Going very still, she stared up at him. "Why are you doing this?" she whispered. "Wasn't embarrassing me in front of all our friends seven years ago enough for you?"

He leaned down until he was no more than four inches from her face. "I tried to apologize. You weren't having any of it."

"Do you think a simple apology could make up for all the other times you were late? Or didn't show up?"

"Don't you think I'd have been there if I could?"

Eden realized they were having the quarrel they should have finished seven years ago. "I think," she began hesitantly, seeking the right words, "that a person makes room in his life for those things that are important to him. That's what I think, Caleb."

He let go of her, thrust his hands in his pockets and paced to the porch railing. "A man has to take care of business. You should know by now that it takes money to keep things going." He gestured to her work on the house.

"A certain amount," she agreed. "But money alone isn't enough. I won't be like my mother. She waited years for my father to have time for her. He never did. And his time ran out."

Caleb turned to her, his face hard. "Are you holding me to account for your father's shortcomings?"

"No. For your own. If I meant so little to you during our engagement that you would put business first, I knew it would be worse when we married. I want to be included in my husband's life. I want to share his worries and his joys."

She felt the futility of explaining. Caleb's father had been like her own—a man engrossed in his work to the exclusion of all else. Caleb had grown up in the same pattern. In many ways their steadfast dedication was admirable, these loyal, hardworking men, but it wasn't the life she wanted.

"Yeah, right," Caleb said when she fell silent. He didn't sound sarcastic, only tired.

She suppressed the pity and concern she felt for him. He had made his bed…

Did he lie in it alone?

That was definitely none of her concern! However, the child was. "I'll bring a bag with me on Sunday," she compromised. "When will you be back?"

"The following Saturday."

"July the Fourth."

He pressed a thumb and finger against the bridge of his nose. "Is it?"

Eden shook her head. He was hopeless. "Will you be home in time to watch the fireworks at the lake?" She knew the country club, next to his house, staged a grand display on the holiday.

"Yes."

"I'll stay at your house until then. Until you get back."

Caleb heard the faint skepticism in the last phrase. Eden didn't believe he'd make it back in time for the festivities with his son. In truth, he thought he'd accepted an invitation to a party at a senator's country house in Virginia. He'd have to check his schedule.

As if it were seven years ago, he heard Eden's voice, saw her grab his pocket calendar and study it. "How many minutes do you have scheduled for me this month, Caleb?" she had demanded, angry when he'd finally gotten back from a trip to Hawaii where they were experimenting with a new variety of coffee.

Eden was spoiled. As much as he admired Jane, he felt

she had never instilled the importance of work into her daughter. Jane had understood that a man had to support his family. Eden had had life too easy....

Well, not recently. Money had been scarce the past few years, according to Sue. Yet Eden still seemed to feel the same about his work.

He gave up trying to figure her out. One thing for sure, he wasn't going to get mixed up with her again. When the summer was over and school started, she was out of his life...for good.

And, while he was thinking about it, he had a few things to say to Sue and his father about nosing into his business.

"Fine," he finally said. "When I'm gone, you stay at the house. Is that a deal?" He let the sarcasm he felt come through.

She hesitated, then nodded. "Yes."

He noticed she didn't smile once or thank him for the job or do anything a person in her position should do. Hell, she should be grateful.... But when had Eden ever done the expected?

Saying good-night over his shoulder, he went down the steps and to his car. All the way home, he prepared what he would say if she ever accused him of not loving Josh the way she'd once accused him of not loving her.

She'd said he'd wanted her, which wasn't the same thing as loving. He felt the rigid heat in his body. That was one thing that hadn't changed, he realized. He still wanted her. This time he knew better than to call it love.

Eden paused over each selection while she packed on Sunday morning. Bathing suits, definitely. She would take Josh to the country club to swim so he could meet other kids.

His birthday was in August. She'd plan a pool party for him at the Remmick house. There was a huge pool there, she remembered. That would be a nice touch right before school resumed.

She chose shorts, slacks and tops, then hesitated over a couple of nice outfits in case they dressed for dinner. She was an employee. She would probably eat in the kitchen. With a wry grimace, she stuck them in, anyway. Jeans, underclothes and a cool nightshirt went in. Finished, she snapped the case closed, picked up her shower-and-makeup kit, then headed downstairs.

Her mother was in the kitchen, lingering over coffee and the Sunday paper. "Are you ready to leave?"

"Yes. I feel like I'm abandoning you, though."

"Let's have lunch Tuesday," Jane suggested. "We'll decide on a restaurant later, someplace where Josh will be comfortable."

"Good. Well, I'm off." She gave her mother a kiss on the cheek and went to her car, feeling rather like Little Red Riding Hood heading off on an unknown adventure.

She drove to the airport and arrived at the gate with a good half hour to spare. Caleb's father hadn't been able to attend, after all. The housekeeper had called and explained that Mr. Remmick was having a "bad day."

Eden had seen him only a few times during the engagement. He'd seemed a bit frail. At one time, he'd probably been much like Caleb, full of ambition and energy, rushing here and there to take care of hot spots in his international trade network.

Caleb had taken over the running after his father's first stroke. She wondered if he ever got tired of it all.

Her thoughts were distracted by the plane's arrival at the gate. While the Jetway was wheeled to the airplane door, she felt a dash of apprehension. What if Josh hated her on sight and resented her for being there instead of his father or grandfather?

She realized that if she were nervous, surely a child thrust into the custody of a stranger would be more so.

The airplane emptied. She had expected Josh to be one of the passengers out last, since he'd have to wait for a flight attendant to escort him. At last she saw a little boy walking with a stewardess. Except for his light hair, he looked exactly like his father.

Ignoring the butterflies in her stomach, Eden managed a smile that was confident and reassuring. It wouldn't do for her to look worried about the situation. That would only alarm him.

She saw his gaze sweep the waiting area. There was no one left waiting but her. The bright expectancy in his brown eyes faded. She recognized the stoic resignation of a child long used to having his hopes dashed.

The boy was a solemn child, dressed like a miniature man in a blue blazer and matching slacks, a white shirt and a blue tie. He looked like one of those children in English dramas who were sent off to boarding schools by parents too busy to cope.

Anger on his behalf swept through her. To let a child face the world alone…

Footsteps sounded behind her. She didn't look around. People were always running like mad in airports.

Josh's face underwent a miraculous change. He smiled as if Christmas and Easter and his birthday had all arrived at once. He pulled away from the hand that held his and ran forward.

A man paused beside her and stooped down. She watched, misty-eyed, as Caleb swept his son into his arms for a bear hug.

Smiling, the flight attendant came forward. "We were told a woman would be picking Josh up. Is that you?"

Eden nodded.

"Could I see your identification?"

Eden showed the woman her driver's license.

"Eden Sommers," the stewardess read aloud. "That's the name. Thank you. Josh was a wonderful passenger, no trouble at all. I hope you'll choose us next time you fly," she said to the boy. With a wave, she hurried off.

"I didn't expect you," Eden said to Caleb.

"I know." He rose and took his son's hand. "I decided to fly in to welcome Josh home. I'm taking the midnight special back."

Eden saw the flurry of emotion on Josh's face—his joy at his father's presence, the return of the stoical expression when he realized he would be leaving again so soon.

"This is Eden Sommers," Caleb said conversationally. He took her arm in his free hand and guided them in the direction of the baggage-claim area. "She's going to be your tutor this summer. Can you say hello?"

"Oui," Josh said. *"Bonjour, mademoiselle."*

"Speak English," Caleb corrected.

Josh furrowed his brow in thought. "Uh, 'allo," he said.

"Very good." Eden smiled brightly. "And hello to you."

"He speaks English very well," Caleb said, sounding defensive on his son's behalf.

"I'm sure he does. However, it's easy to get mixed up a bit when you're in strange surroundings. Once when I was in France, I got lost and suddenly couldn't remember how to ask directions back to my hotel."

Josh shot her a surprised glance, then smiled shyly at her.

Caleb chatted with his son while they waited for the luggage. His gaze lighted on Eden occasionally, and he'd study her as if wondering about her. His glances caused tremors to rush along her nerves. He was still the most attractive man she'd ever seen.

In another half hour they were on the road in Eden's car. She drove. Josh sat in front so he could see the landmarks. She pointed them out to him and told him amusing stories about the town. "The Great Fire of 1871 started in a barn belonging to Patrick O'Leary. Mrs. O'Leary's cow kicked over a lantern and set the straw on fire, so the story goes. I guess it didn't feel like being milked that morning."

"Or maybe Mrs. O'Leary had cold hands and the cow didn't like that," Caleb suggested. He spoke over her shoulder, startling her.

"Is your seat belt fastened?" she demanded, as tingles ran down her neck.

"No."

"Well, put it on. Otherwise I'll have to stop the car until you do," she threatened, when he didn't comply immediately.

To her delight, Josh grinned as his dad sat back and buckled in. "The driver is boss in an automobile," she explained to him. "Remember that when you have a car."

A soft snort issued from the back. She ignored it.

"Here we are," she announced when she turned into the drive to the elegant brick mansion. "Did you see the red bird that just flew by, Josh?"

"*Oui*, uh, yes, *mademoiselle*, uh…"

"Her name is Miss Sommers," Caleb said from the back seat.

Eden flashed him a mind-your-own-business look in the rearview mirror, then spoke to Josh. "Call me Eden. All my friends do."

She smiled at the solemn little boy, who had listened to every word she said with an almost adult concentration. "The red bird—the cardinal—is a symbol of good luck," she continued.

Josh looked hopeful. "It is?" he asked in his careful, accented English.

"Yes," she continued. "Good fortune seems to be smiling on you today. First there was the surprise when your father met you at the airport. And now you'll get to see your grandfather—"

"*Bon-papa?*" Josh interrupted.

"Not *Bon-papa*. Grandfather Remmick," Caleb said. "He calls his other grandfather *Bon-papa*," he explained to Eden.

"I see. Do you remember this grandfather, Josh? Grandfather Remmick?"

"I—I think so."

"It's been over a year since Josh was here," Caleb told her. "Park in the front by the steps."

Eden tried to contain her anger over the fact that Caleb had been going to leave his child with virtual strangers.

It was none of her business, she reminded herself ruthlessly. Josh seemed a very mature, very bright little boy. She knew kids could accept the most bizarre life-style without undue harm, as long as they felt loved. That was the key.

Caleb loved his child. The fact that he had made the effort to be there upon Josh's arrival indicated that much.

She wondered how different her life might have been if he'd cared enough to make an effort for her. Not that it mattered now. All that was in the past. She had one purpose—to make Josh's transition to his new life as painless as possible.

But it might not be an easy task, she admitted, stopping in front of the handsome brick mansion. Once, she'd thought this house would be *her* home. It had belonged to Caleb's mother, and he had inherited it the year before he and Eden had met. They had planned to live there.

For a second, she gripped the steering wheel, forcing her shaky emotions to obey her will. A big help she would be to Josh if she couldn't control her own anxieties about being there. More than ever, she felt it had been foolish on her part to take this job.

The front door opened and a servant with red hair and a beard hurried down the steps. The occupants of the car climbed out.

"Josh, do you remember Henry? He stays with Grandfather Remmick and helps him with his wheelchair," Caleb said.

Josh peered closely at the man and nodded shyly, then smiled. Eden realized Caleb was refreshing the child's memory, helping him feel at home.

"Hello, Josh," Henry said heartily. His grin squeezed his blue eyes into merry slits. "You're going to be surprised when you see your grandfather," he predicted. So saying, he grabbed a suitcase, stuck it under his arm, picked up two more and headed inside.

Caleb handed Eden's toiletries case to his son. Josh looked surprised, then pleased. Caleb grabbed her large suitcase and one of Josh's. The son marched proudly up the steps beside him, his eyes going to Caleb's face often.

Josh adored his father.

The knowledge hurt in ways Eden hadn't expected. The child's love echoed her own adoration of Caleb. And then had come the painful realization—which she'd been unable to ignore the night of their engagement party—that he didn't feel the same way about her.

"Coming?"

She jerked out of her introspection and nodded. Caleb's eyes were dark and probing as he watched her climb the steps. He waited until she was in the hall before stepping into the house behind her and closing the door.

"Up the stairs," he said.

Henry, she saw, was at the top. She and Josh hurried after him.

The room across from the stairs was definitely a boy's room. The furniture was built in, with two twin-size sleeping areas at right angles to each other on a middle level. Under the beds were drawers and cabinets to hold clothes and toys. Up in a corner, on the highest level, was a platform with wooden railings all around it. A ladder gave access to it.

"*La cabane*...the tree house!" Josh exclaimed. "Am I big enough to go there?" He looked anxiously at Caleb.

His father smiled. "Stand over here and let's measure you."

Josh put Eden's case down carefully and dashed over to a tape measure mounted on the wall. Caleb marked his height. Josh peered at the pencil line anxiously. A big smile spread over his face.

Caleb tousled his hair. "You made it. I thought you would. Henry and I put up the ladder last week."

Henry set Josh's bags on a bench along one wall. The bench was beside a desk. Above it, bookcases filled with books rose to the ceiling.

Eden glanced at some of the titles. There were high school books as well as children's adventure stories, all with the look of having been well read. She realized the room had been Caleb's in his youth. It opened a window into his psyche.

She turned to find him watching her. Josh was in the tree house. Henry had left, apparently taking her two cases with him.

"Where am I to stay?" she asked. Her voice sounded strained to her ears. She hoped Caleb didn't notice.

"In the next room. There's a connecting door." He pointed to a door standing open in the wall opposite the desk. "Josh, take care," he called. "I'm going to show Eden to her room."

"*Oui*...yes, I will."

She followed Caleb into a pleasant corner bedroom with tall windows on two walls. The view was magnificent. She could see Lake Michigan in the distance and the country club grounds in the other direction.

The four-poster bed had blue satin curtains draped in swags from the ceiling and falling to each side of it. A blue-and-gold brocaded silk sofa, with two small tables in front and reading lamps on each side, formed a sitting area. A lady's secretary with a glass front and a fold-down writing surface stood between two windows. Her luggage stood beside a maple armoire.

"Will it do?" a sardonic voice inquired.

Caleb stood directly behind her. Eden became instantly aware of him and his warmth, which radiated over her back. A yearning to lean against him and feel him take her once more into his arms rioted through her. She'd loved him so....

"Eden?"

She stepped away and turned to him. Her throat had closed, and it was impossible to speak.

"Regrets?" he inquired. He swept a hand out, indicating his home and all that went with it. "This would have been yours, all yours. Everything I had—"

"Not everything," she denied. "Not the important things."

A look of pure fury flickered through his eyes. She wrapped her arms over her chest to hold herself intact from its force.

"What more was there?"

"A place in your heart and in your life," she said softly, sorrowfully. "You never planned a place for me in your life."

"You *were* my life."

She shook her head. "Try to make room for your son, Caleb. Josh needs you."

Chapter Four

"Mr. Remmick is waiting in the study," Henry announced, breaking the thread of tension between them. "Lunch will be served there."

Eden breathed a sigh of relief at the interruption. She didn't want to quarrel with Caleb. How he ran his life was up to him, not her. Having made her feelings clear—in her usual mode of operating, with one foot in her mouth—she would say no more.

While Caleb went to collect Josh, she followed Henry down the stairs and into a room she remembered very well. Two leather sofas flanked a fireplace, which now displayed a pot of ferns instead of a fire. Mr. Remmick stood in front of the French doors that opened onto a view of sweeping lawns and the golf course next door.

He smiled and came toward her, with a cane in his hand but no other sign of his stroke that she could detect. "Eden, it's good to see you again. You're lovelier than I remembered."

"Thank you. You're looking very well yourself," she said. "I had assumed you would still be in a wheelchair."

His eyes, as dark as his son's and grandson's, twinkled at her. "I wanted to surprise everyone."

"You've certainly surprised me," Caleb said from behind them. "I didn't realize you were walking. Josh, say hello to Grandfather Remmick," he coaxed his son. They crossed the room.

Josh stepped forward and held out his hand. "How do you do, sir?" he said in his careful English.

"Fine, thank you," the older man replied. They shook hands. "Tell me about your trip. Was it a rough crossing?"

Eden caught the gleam of pride on Caleb's face. His son showed many signs of being well brought up. Josh was polite, almost to a fault. She would have to teach him to laugh.

"Shall we start lunch?" Mr. Remmick inquired when Josh ended his recounting of his journey. "Mrs. O'Leary promised to make something special for us. I thought we'd eat in here on trays."

Josh's eyes opened wide. He darted a questioning glance at Eden. She grinned and winked, as if they shared a joke. He put a hand over his mouth as a giggle erupted. Eden laughed, too.

"Have I missed something?" Mr. Remmick asked.

Caleb answered. "I suspect it has something to do with Mrs. O'Leary's cow. Eden told Josh the story on the way here."

Quickly composing himself, Josh asked, "Was it *her* cow?"

"We'll have to ask," Mr. Remmick suggested. When the housekeeper entered, he spoke to her. "My grandson wants to know if it was your cow, Mrs. O'Leary, that set off the Great Fire in Chicago a hundred or so years ago."

The housekeeper, a widow, was short, rotund and as red-headed as her brother, Henry. She placed a tray with lemonade and glasses on a low table and counted on her fingers as she spoke. "It was my dear husband's great-great-great-great-grandmother's cow, so it's said in the O'Leary family."

"C'est magnifique!" Josh exclaimed enthusiastically.

The adults laughed at his relish for the adventure. It was clear he wished his own ancestors had such a claim to fame.

"Actually, it was good for the city," Mr. Remmick observed. "It cleared out a lot of flimsy housing, which was replaced with brick and stone."

"A rather drastic form of urban renewal," Caleb murmured.

Henry wheeled a cart into the study and set up individual table trays, which were inlaid with a pattern of dark and light woods. Eden realized they could also be used for game boards.

"Josh plays a fair game of chess," Caleb told his father. "You might challenge him one evening if you feel up to it."

"Only if he'll play a couple of warm-up games first. I haven't played in years." Mr. Remmick smiled at Josh.

"I will, sir," Josh promised.

An hour passed in genial conversation as Josh became reacquainted with his American grandfather. Eden learned that the boy had lived in a house next to the beach and that his French grandparents had kept goats.

"They mow the grass," Josh explained solemnly. He looked out the window at the well-tended lawn. "How many do you have?"

"Well, I use a gardener. He mows with a machine," Mr. Remmick admitted. "It doesn't sound near as much fun as goats."

As she listened, Eden began to plan Josh's education.

He needed to become thoroughly familiar with American life in order to feel comfortable at school. Three months would be plenty of time to bring him on board, so to speak.

When the boy covered a yawn for the third time, she realized he had probably been up since before dawn.

"Josh needs a nap," she said at a pause in the conversation. When the two men looked at her in surprise, she gave them her schoolteacher smile—the one that said she was in charge. "Caleb, why don't you read him a story? I noticed a Peter Rabbit book on the shelf in his room. Was it yours at one time?"

"Yes." Caleb rose and lifted his son in his arms. "Come on, sport. The boss lady has spoken."

Josh stole a glance at Eden, then his father, not sure how to take this wry remark.

Caleb grinned at him. "One of the first things a man needs to learn in life is never argue with a woman. They'll win every time, one way or the other."

"Because we're usually right," Eden called to him as he swung his son up onto his shoulders.

"Huh," Caleb snorted. "Watch the doorframe," he cautioned his son as they left the room.

"You handled that very well," Mr. Remmick observed.

Eden tried to look innocent as she met his knowing eyes, but heat crept into her cheeks. She had shamelessly manipulated Caleb, forcing him to spend some quiet time with his son. It seemed to her that the father needed to be taught his role as much as Josh needed to brush up on his English.

"Do you think my grandson will adjust to American life?" the older man asked, a worried frown appearing on his face.

"Yes. Josh is obviously very bright. He's mature for his age and very self-possessed." He got the last from his father, she suspected. Caleb never seemed to need anyone.

"Will the other children laugh at his accent?"

"I doubt it. At the academy, we have several children whose first language is something other than English. They don't seem to have any trouble." She smiled reassuringly at the older man. "Wealthy people tend to marry internationally more than most other groups."

There was a moment of silence. Then, "Marry my son, Eden," Mr. Remmick said.

She stared at him, waiting for the punch line. He had to be joking.

He didn't smile. "He needs you as much as my grandson does…perhaps more."

"Mr. Remmick, if you and Sue plotted this—"

"We did," he admitted.

Her heart danced around in her chest at his confession. She didn't know what to say. "It can never be."

"Why?"

Out in the hall, a grandfather clock played the Westminster chimes before striking the hour. She counted the bongs. Three o'clock. "Our time has passed. Too much has happened—"

"The only time I ever saw Caleb truly happy was during those few months with you. When he came home from a trip, he was always whistling. There was joy in his eyes. He'd go to the telephone and call you. It was the very first thing he did."

Eden felt only pain at hearing this. She got up and paced to the window. In the distance, she watched a foursome line up on the golf course and tee off.

"Give him something to live for," Mr. Remmick requested.

She closed her eyes as tears threatened, and shook her head. "I'm here to help Josh. I'll do that to the best of my ability. Caleb is a grown man. He has to decide his own course in life. No one can do it for him." She opened her eyes and stared at the peaceful scene in the distance.

Mr. Remmick sighed heavily. "It was my fault…the breakup between you and Caleb. I caused it."

She turned to him, astounded by his words.

He gave her a sad smile. "I rarely saw my son when he was growing up. I was…too busy. When Caleb came into the business, it was a gift—a second chance. He was brilliant, better than I ever was. He could go into a situation and size it up at a glance. He became my legs, my alter ego. We grew close."

"With business as the center of your lives," she said, seeing the picture.

"Yes." He gripped the handle of his cane and rose slowly to his feet. "When you came into his life, I was jealous, although I wouldn't have admitted it at the time. I saw my place being taken by a slip of a girl. Hormones, I thought. I could accept that, but you demanded more. I didn't want to lose my son, so I fought back."

"How? What do you mean?"

"I gave him more work, stressed the need for him to go on trips and check things out in person. The more he turned to you, the more I pressured him with his responsibilities to the company. For a man, it's a strong argument."

"I know."

"I was wrong." He came toward her and leaned wearily on the cane. "Wrong," he repeated. "I hope you can forgive me."

"Of course I can," she murmured.

"Don't be so quick about it. I need to suffer for my sins."

"I'm sure you have, or else you couldn't have said what you did."

"Caleb suffered more. And so did you." He touched her arm with a trembling hand. "Sue said there has been no one else in your life, although she's introduced you to several young men." There was a question in the comment.

The tears pressed closer to the surface. She blinked them back. "I've been too busy to think of things like that," she said, putting on a bright smile.

"Caleb married on the rebound. So did Antoinette, I think. She'd found her fiancé with another woman a week before the wedding."

"How terrible for her," Eden said, her heart going out to the woman. And to Caleb. If he'd been unhappy…

"Ahem," Henry said, coming into the room. "Are you ready to lie down?" he asked his employer. "It's been a rather long day."

"My wet nurse," Mr. Remmick grumbled, but with affection. He left the room with a limp that was more pronounced than earlier.

Eden wrapped her arms across her chest as if to ward off the too-ready emotions. Mr. Remmick had touched her heart. She saw him as a lonely old man, one who had devoted himself to work and now realized he had little to show for it at the end of his life except for an empty house and more money than he could spend.

Perhaps with Josh there, life wouldn't be so barren for him. Maybe Caleb could be convinced to let someone else do the running, to take more time for his father and son.

She sighed, knowing it was none of her business and knowing, too, that she would do whatever she possibly could to make that happen. *Fools rush in…*

The house seemed eerily quiet. She decided to go to her room and unpack. It was time she settled in.

The task had been partially done, she found. Her clothes were neatly arranged in the huge closet. She stored her lingerie in the armoire, noting that the drawers were lined with scented paper. She found she had her own bathroom, with a whirlpool tub as well as a shower with a marble shelf. She unpacked her toiletries case.

Finished, she wondered what she should do now. She wasn't sleepy at all. A knock at her door set her heart to pounding.

Caleb was waiting in the hall when she opened it. "I thought you might like a tour of the house," he said.

"That would be nice." She was surprised at his perception.

He led the way to a door at the end of the hall. "The servants' stairs."

They went up to the third floor.

"This used to be the servants' and children's quarters back at the turn of the century. The rooms are used for storage now. If there are any toys up here you think Josh would like, you're welcome to take them."

She exclaimed over a dollhouse set up in one room, complete with furniture, and tiny people to inhabit the ornate interior.

"I'd have loved this," she said, peering through the clear plastic covering.

There were child-size rockers, doll buggies and a carved baby cradle. She paused and touched the cradle, setting it to rocking back and forth.

"My mother's stuff," Caleb explained. "This was her childhood home. And her mother's before her."

"How old is the house?"

"Late nineteenth century. My great-grandfather was one of the meat-packing kings Upton Sinclair wrote about."

"Rather brutally," she pointed out.

Caleb nodded. "A ruthless time run by ruthless men."

"Is it any different now?" She met his gaze levelly.

His eyes narrowed. "Do you think me ruthless?"

Eden studied his expression for a minute. He didn't give any emotion away, but she sensed the tension in him...as if the answer she gave was important to him. Not that she believed that, but still, there was something… A shiver of apprehension ran over her. She considered her reply carefully.

"I've always thought you were an honorable man."

He frowned. "I don't think that answers my question. Do you think I'm ruthless?"

She shrugged and walked out of the room. He caught her in the dim, silent hall, putting a hand on her arm.

"Dammit, answer me!"

He wouldn't let it rest, she saw, yet she didn't want to discuss her assessment of him. "What difference does it make? I'm sure you're not the least interested in my opinion."

"I asked, didn't I?" He spoke in a low tone that was all the more menacing for its quiet control.

"Then, yes, I think you're ruthless."

"In what way?"

She started toward the next doorway. He let her go and followed, his hands in his pockets, his eyes never leaving her.

"You never let anything get in the way of your interests…."

Her voice trailed off as she remembered he'd flown in to be with Josh for one day, although doing so must have played havoc with his schedule.

"That isn't true," she corrected herself. "It must have been hard to take your one day of rest between the Senate hearings and come meet Josh. I'm glad you did. Did you see his face when he saw you?" she asked gently. "Having you there meant the world to him."

Caleb nodded grimly. "But will he remember that when tomorrow comes and I'm gone again? Or will he hate me, as you did, for only giving him bits and pieces of my life?"

She started to reply defensively, but saw he wasn't taunting her. He seemed genuinely interested in her answer.

Taking a deep breath, she told him the truth. "There is no such thing as quality time, Caleb. The events in a child's life, either wonderful or frightful, happen so fleetingly. You're either there for them or you're not. Things can't be planned or repeated for your benefit."

"Josh seems to do okay."

"He holds in a lot of his emotions. I saw that at the airport."

"Did you?"

"Yes. Look at his life. His mother died when he was three. His other grandparents apparently filled the void. Now they're gone, and he's in new surroundings. Your father's health isn't all that good. Who is going to be your son's North Star, the steady point he needs to guide him through life? Who is the one person he can go to in times of joy or fear and know that he or she will be there for him?"

She returned his hard gaze with a steady one of her own.

"Who, Caleb?" she demanded softly.

The grandfather clock sounded the half hour from the hallway far below. It filled the silence between them.

"I will," Caleb said at last.

"When?"

His face darkened. "As soon as I can get things straightened out."

"When will that be? This year? The next? Josh might not be there when you decide you have time for him. Maybe his role model will be the tough kid down on the corner who deals dope. What then?"

"You don't just stab a guy, Eden. You put the knife in and twist." Instead of being angry, he seemed weary. He pushed a hand through the dark waves of his hair, his chest moving in a deep sigh.

Eden felt herself softening toward him. He was worried about Josh. She knew he had a load of responsibilities. It occurred to her that Caleb tried to be too many things to too many people. He stretched himself too thin.

"Set your priorities," she advised, but with a compassion she didn't want to feel. "No one is indispensable, no matter how much we might think we are. If you died tomorrow, who would take your place in your business… or with your son?"

"Who made you the all-wise one?" he asked her with only a slight overtone of sarcasm.

She smiled rather sheepishly. "Sorry. I'll get off my soapbox," she promised. She walked on.

They peered into two more rooms. Both were empty. Caleb led the way down another set of stairs, at the front of the house. They came out on the second floor.

"The master suite," he said, opening a door and beckoning for her to enter.

She stepped in hesitantly, wondering about Mr. Remmick. But there was no one in the room. As soon as she saw Caleb's suit jacket tossed carelessly over a chair, she realized her error. Heat flared inside her. She hoped it wasn't reflected on her face.

"This is your room?" she asked, nervous about being there, about being alone with him.

"Yes," he said coolly. "Did you think it was my father's?"

"You said the master suite."

"My father moved downstairs, into what used to be called the morning room, after his first stroke. It's next to the study."

"I see." She quickly glanced around the room, then headed into the hall again. "Are the rest of these rooms guest rooms?"

"Yes. There are three more bedrooms, besides yours and the one Josh has."

"Umm," she said, hurrying toward the stairs.

The image of his room lingered in her mind. The bed was king-size. Of course. There was a sofa in one corner and comfortable chairs. Books and magazines. A wall cabinet with a television and stereo equipment. A bathroom door stood open at one side. The whole suite made a very comfortable retreat.

With this vision, she saw another…a vision of them alone in there after the day was over, talking, sharing laughter…making love.

An ache pierced her chest. It should have been her. It could have been. She forced herself to blank out the fantasy.

"This is the dining room," he said, catching up with her in the lower hall. He pointed out the spacious formal living room, the kitchen and pantry area, the den to his father's room, then led her back to the study. "Mrs. O'Leary has her apartment over the garage. Henry has a cottage on the grounds."

"Your home is very nice," she said. Something else seemed called for. "Spacious."

His mouth flattened into an angry line. "Relax, Eden. I'm not about to attack you, either for what you said upstairs or…"

"Or?" she challenged bravely.

"Or because I can't control my baser instincts."

He held her gaze and wouldn't let go. Tension arced between them, defying either's willpower or common sense. Flames erupted within. She saw them reflected in his eyes.

He wanted her. Passionately.

And, heaven help her, she felt the same! The hunger between them was as strong as it had been the first night they'd met. It wasn't something that pleased her.

He moved closer to her, not touching, but almost.

"No," she said.

"No?" His voice was a rough murmur of desire, flowing darkly into the hidden recesses of her soul. "Your eyes say different."

"They lie. I—I don't want you...not like this...."

He closed his eyes and spun away, standing with his back to her while he fought for control. It unnerved her to see him like this. She had always thought of Caleb as being coolly in command. He had always been in charge of their tempestuous affair, the one to call a halt to their wild kisses. He'd been the one who had taken them beyond kisses....

She crossed to a chair on weak legs and sat down. Pulling a pillow into her lap, she hugged it against her aching chest.

"I had wondered," he said huskily, "how I would feel upon seeing you again. I didn't expect this."

"Why not?" she foolishly asked. "It was this way the first time we met."

He went to a bar built into a bank of bookcases. From a small refrigerator, he removed a bottle of wine and poured them each a glass of white zinfandel. After giving one to her, he took his own and sat in the chair opposite hers, across the coffee table.

A smile played at the corners of his mouth. His gaze lazily roamed her face, stopping at her eyes, her mouth, dropping down to her throat, her breasts.

"You're still the same," he said, amusement lighting his eyes. "You never hid your feelings, not from the first."

She sipped the cool wine, letting its tart flavor soothe her dry throat. It was her favorite wine. She wondered if Caleb had remembered. Glancing into his eyes, she knew that he had.

She replied to her thoughts, not his statement. "I shouldn't have taken this job. Sue and your father..." She stopped before she betrayed them.

"Planned this whole thing?" he concluded for her. "I guessed as much. There were too many coincidences."

"Yes." Misery settled over her. Three months. Would she fall in love with him again during that time?

His expression hardened, as if he'd just remembered their mutual past and why he hated her. "It shouldn't be a problem. The times I'm here, you'll be free to go home."

She nodded and sipped the wine, wishing she were anyplace but here, in this house they would have shared as husband and wife.

The chimes sounded and the clock struck four.

The silence enclosed them in an illusory peace. Eden sighed. When Caleb gave her a sharp glance, she realized how shaky she had sounded. She felt that way—tremulous and uncertain, the way she'd felt at nineteen, in love for the first time and not sure of him or herself or life.

If she were going to succeed at this job, she had to maintain an emotional distance, she realized. She set the pillow aside, put the glass on the table and rose.

"It's about time for Josh to wake up. I'll go check on him." She quickly left the room and its false serenity.

She found Josh lying on his comforter in the tree house, looking out the window toward the small lake on the country club grounds. He gave her a shy smile.

"My dad said I could sleep up here for my nap," he told her proudly. "May I sleep here tonight, too?"

She noted the bottom rail was low enough that he wouldn't slip under it and fall off in his sleep. "That depends," she told him solemnly. "Do you walk in your sleep?"

"*Non*...no, I do not think so."

"Good. I'll speak to your father about it before he leaves."

She noted the careful blanking of his expression at the mention of Caleb's departure. "Are you hungry?" she went on.

"I'm…" He paused. "I'm…*soif?*"

"Thirsty."

"Oui."

"I'm thirsty," she repeated.

He caught on at once. "I'm thirsty."

"Very good. Come. We'll find Mrs. O'Leary, ask about a drink and find out when dinner is served."

The evening skipped past like a stone over water, disappearing in a moment, it seemed. After the meal they played a round-robin of chess. Josh beat his grandfather. Caleb beat Eden. Then Caleb and Josh played to a stalemate while the other two looked on.

At nine, Eden stood. "Josh must go to bed now. It's midnight or later on his internal clock."

Caleb rose and took his son's hand. "I'll supervise his bath tonight," he volunteered. He shot Eden a mocking smile. "I don't want to miss any fleeting moments."

She grinned back, not at all abashed by his reminder of her scolding. At least he was taking it to heart.

"Uh, Eden, the bed?" Josh said, his dark eyes anxious.

A warm sensation seized her heart. He had claimed her as his friend. "Josh wants to sleep in the tree house tonight. I told him we would check with you."

Caleb thought it over. "I think the tree house should be for special occasions, like when you have friends over. You may nap there in summer, but your bed is the proper place to sleep."

The child accepted the decision without protest. Eden noted that he hadn't really expected a different one. She resolved to think of something she might suggest so she could let him talk her into changing her mind.

"I'll come up and turn back the bed," she said.

She followed the two males up the stairs. "There's a secret staircase at the end of the hall," she announced casually.

"Really?" Josh gave his dad a questioning look.

"Well, umm, yes, I guess you could say that," Caleb agreed. "Maybe Eden will show it to you tomorrow."

Josh nodded. He glanced at Eden over his shoulder. She nodded, too, promising that she would. He smiled his quiet, shy smile.

She smiled in turn, feeling relief. Now he had something to look forward to while Caleb was gone. She would make an adventure out of it. They'd explore the whole house, attic to basement.

"Would you prefer a shower or a bath in the tub?" she heard Caleb ask while she crossed to the beds.

"A shower," Josh promptly answered, then added, *"s'il vous plaît."*

"Please," Caleb said.

"A shower, please," Josh repeated.

Eden noted that the book Caleb had read to his son earlier was lying on the twin bed nearest the windows. She turned the covers back on that one. Going through the closets, she found that his neat little suits had been hung up, but the rest of his clothing was still in the suitcases. Another task for tomorrow.

She found pajamas and laid them on the bed.

"Ears, Josh," Caleb called out from the bathroom, over the sound of running water. "Use soap."

A smile settled on her mouth. Caleb as a father had never been one of her fantasies, but it was one that she found endearing. He had a lot of patience with his son.

It wasn't a trait he'd shown to her, she realized. The smile faded. That was one thing she didn't need—to start spinning dreams about Caleb in a role other than employer.

She was the tutor, that was all. And only for the summer.

After Josh was tucked in bed, she picked up a volume she had already chosen from the bookcase. "This is an ad-

venture story about a boy and his dog, called Lassie. Have
you heard it?"

"*Non, mad*...no."

"I thought we might read a chapter each night," Eden
suggested.

From the corner of her eye, she saw Caleb pause, then
nod in approval. To her surprise, he took a chair as she sat
on the end of the bed and opened the book. She hadn't
expected to have a grown-up in the audience.

After clearing her throat, she began the story.

When she'd finished the allotted chapter, Josh was
sleepy eyed. His father was sprawled in the rocking chair,
his legs stretched out and crossed at the ankles. His own
eyes were closed.

Eden stood and checked that Josh was covered. The air-
conditioning made the room rather chilly at night. She
paused beside Caleb, hating to wake him.

He opened his eyes suddenly, catching her staring at
him. He stood and stretched, then held the door open for
her to precede him into the hall. He closed the door quietly.

They started down the steps. "You seem to know a lot
about children," he mentioned.

"I'm studying child psychology in my spare time. When
I finish my thesis, I'll have a master's degree in it."

"You always wanted children," he said.

From the bottom of the steps, she looked over her
shoulder at him, troubled by the yearning that rose in her.

"Don't get any ideas," he told her in a harsher tone.
"You and I... It was over a long time ago."

"I know." She smiled slightly. "But one can't help wondering what might have been."

She left him standing there, looking shocked by her
statement.

Chapter Five

Mr. Remmick was in the study when Eden entered. There were two coffee urns and a few cups on a tray. "Would you pour, Eden?" he asked.

"Of course." She sat on the sofa behind the coffee table and began to do so. "Cream or sugar?" she asked the older man.

"Neither. The smaller pot is decaffeinated. I'll take that."

"I'll have regular," Caleb said, walking into the cozy room. "I'll work on the plane going back."

She stifled a protest. He looked so tired. His eyes were bloodshot, and a weary frown creased his forehead. Guilt ate at her. She really had no right to interfere in his life.

But when had that ever stopped her from doing what she thought was right? she questioned wryly. "Will you call Josh when you get a chance?" She handed Caleb a cup and met his dark gaze.

"Yes."

"What time? So I'll know when to have him at the house," she added when he raised that expressive eyebrow at her.

"Let's see. There's an hour's difference in time. If I call at ten p.m., that would be nine here. Is that all right?"

She ignored the sardonic undertone. "Fine. What night?"

"I'll try to call every night."

"Every night?"

"Don't look so skeptical," Caleb advised. "Stranger things have happened. I don't know exactly what my schedule will be, but I'll try to squeeze Josh in."

"That's very commendable," she said in the most sincere voice she could muster.

Mr. Remmick looked from one to the other as they verbally sparred. A smile played over his mouth, then was gone. "About the contract on the Colombian coffee," he said.

With the conversation delving into business matters, even the amount of money involved—which was staggering—Eden felt like an interloper. "Shall I leave?" she asked at one point.

"No," Caleb said equably. "Unless the talk of business bores you to tears. We wouldn't want that, would we, Father?"

"Not at all," Mr. Remmick remarked.

So she stayed. She was amazed at the complications involved in buying and selling something so simple as coffee. She stared into the steam rising from her cup. Tariffs, international treaties, warlords and a host of other things were involved.

At eleven, Henry appeared at the study door. "The car is here," he said.

"Time to hit the road," Caleb said to his father. He stood and looked at Eden thoughtfully.

She stood, feeling self-conscious.

"Josh is in your hands," he said. "You have the final word on him and his activities over anyone else, including me. Do you understand?"

"Yes." She realized he was telling her he had absolute faith in her decisions. "Thank you," she said formally.

He nodded. Turning to his father, he touched him on the shoulder. "Take care or Eden will have you toeing the line, too," he said, giving her a mocking grin as he walked toward the door.

"I'll appeal to her kind heart," Mr. Remmick said.

Caleb paused at the door. "Does she have one?"

"Oh, yes," his father assured him. "She most assuredly does."

Eden felt heat rise up her neck and into her face as Caleb looked at her once more. An enigmatic smile touched the corners of his mouth. "I think you may be right, sir." He left.

A moment of quiet followed the departure of the limousine.

Henry returned to the door and gave Mr. Remmick a questioning look. The older man rose. Leaning heavily on his cane, he limped to the door. He paused there the way Caleb had and looked at her with the same mysterious smile. She realized how much they resembled each other—father and son and grandson.

Three of a kind, she thought. Affection lit her face as she smiled back at Caleb's father. Between them, they'd probably manage to break her heart all over again.

Eden woke with the sun shining through the sheer curtains at the windows. She threw back the covers and headed for the shower. There was a lot to do today. But slowly. She didn't want to give Josh a case of cultural overload.

After she was dressed, she knocked on the connecting bedroom door.

"Enter," he called in his careful English.

She found him in the tree house, playing with several tiny trucks and cars. He had lined them up on the railing like the traffic on the expressway around the city. Dressed in shorts and a white shirt, he gave her a quick smile and waited, as if for orders.

"Good, you're dressed. Let's have breakfast, then we'll unpack your stuff and put it away."

He came down the ladder with careful concentration. Such a serious little boy.

She noted his foreign-looking sandals. Hmm, some shopping might be in order. She'd see after they unpacked.

When they finished their cereal and fruit, Josh excused himself and came to her side of the table. "Eden?" he said in a low voice.

"Yes?"

"You won't forget the secret stairs?" He looked at her anxiously.

Her heart went out to him. "No, indeed. We'll go up them on the way back to your room, shall we?"

He nodded, his eyes shining.

She led the way to the end of the hall and opened the door, then stood aside so he could enter. He hesitated. "Was anyone murdered here?" he asked.

"Where did you learn about murder?" Eden asked. She wasn't surprised at the question. Children loved mystery and mayhem.

"On the television."

"Ah, yes." She smiled at him. "I don't think anyone was killed on these stairs, but we can ask Henry or Mrs. O'Leary about it at lunch."

The stairs were wonderfully dark and a little creaky.

Josh slipped his hand into hers as they climbed to the second floor. She showed him the door to the hallway, then they went up the rest of the way, pausing at the third story to look down the hall there, then going all the way up to the attic.

The attic was a disappointment, totally empty and with hardly any cobwebs to lend atmosphere. They went back to Josh's room and began putting his clothing away.

Eden added a trip to the mall to their afternoon plans. To fit in with the local crowd, he needed sneakers and jeans and T-shirts. His blue shorts and white shirts seemed like a uniform.

"Did you go to school in Martinique, Josh?"

"*Mais oui.* I had a tutor there, too. Brother Sebastian held class for four of us. We were too far from town to go to a real school."

"I see. Did he teach in English or French?"

"French in the morning. We had English every afternoon."

Eden was pleased. That explained his wide vocabulary. And probably his manners. Josh had been raised with some rather old-fashioned discipline. He exhibited the traits of a child who spent most of his time with adults. She would like to see him display more spontaneity, however, and control his emotions without suppressing them, which was what she suspected he did.

The day went as planned. They explored the house thoroughly, then the grounds. That afternoon they went to that most American of places, the shopping mall.

They bought clothes and shoes, then had warm chocolate-chip cookies on the way out.

"That was a grand place," Josh told her on the way home. He brushed a speck of dust off his new high-top sneakers.

Eden laughed. "Yes, it was." When they turned into the

drive, she asked, "What would you like to do now? We have over an hour before dinner."

He thought seriously before answering. "There is a lake near the house." He pronounced *house* as *'ouse* and had some trouble with the *th* sound.

"Hmm," she said with a slight frown. "I don't think we should go there."

Disappointment flicked in his eyes, but he said nothing.

"Of course, it might be fun."

"Oh, yes, it would be," he said quickly.

"But we might get hit by a golf ball."

"Oh."

"But if we were careful…" She paused, as if mulling it over. "What do you think?"

"Moi?" he said in surprise. His expression was earnest, not facetious, the way Americans usually said the word.

"Yes, you. Do you think we could watch out for golf balls?"

"Mais oui," he said, excitement shining in his eyes.

"You've convinced me," she said. "We'll take your clothes in and let your grandfather know where we're going."

"Très bien," he said, sighing happily.

She tousled his hair, even though she knew kids hated when adults did that. They had to learn to accept some grown-up traits that were annoying.

Inside, Josh surprised her by inviting his grandfather to join them. "We will watch the golf balls for you," he promised.

Mr. Remmick was touched. "I don't move very quickly," he pointed out apologetically.

"That's no problem," Eden said swiftly.

"Then, yes, I'd love to go. Henry, are you up for a walk? He's not as young as he used to be," Mr. Remmick said in an aside to his grandson.

Josh nodded solemnly. "I am not, either."

They made it to the lake without incident. There, they found a school of minnows in the shallows. When Eden took off her shoes and started wading, Josh looked at her with envy.

"Don't you want to join me?" she asked.

He looked at his grandfather.

"I will." Mr. Remmick sat down on a rock and pulled his shoes off. Astonished, Josh did the same. Henry declined when invited to join them.

"Someone's got to show some sense in this crowd," he declared.

All in all, they had a nice time, Eden thought later that night. They'd returned, washed up and had a casual supper in the study. She liked that better than eating in the formal dining room, as they had the previous night.

The three of them watched a Disney movie; then she and Josh discussed it while he took his bath and prepared for bed. They read another chapter in their adventure story.

At nine-thirty, she closed the book and leaned over Josh. She bent and kissed him on the cheek, so naturally, she didn't even think about it. "Good night."

"Good night," he murmured, more than half-asleep.

He hadn't mentioned his father all day, she noted. It was as if the child had closed off all memory of him until the man actually reappeared. A denial mechanism, she decided.

If Josh didn't think about Caleb, he wouldn't be hurt because his dad wasn't there. Anger had her clenching her jaw. Caleb had forgotten to call.

In all fairness, he hadn't promised he would…like all the times he'd promised her, then had failed to do so.

As if to mock her, the phone in the hall rang at that moment. She grabbed up the receiver. "Hello." Did she sound breathless?

"Hello, Eden. Is Josh asleep yet?"

"No. I'll get him." She held out the phone. "Your dad wants to tell you good-night."

Stardust danced in Josh's eyes as he took the phone. Eden had to look away from his happiness.

"Dad, you should see my new shoes," he said as soon as he returned Caleb's greeting. "Sir? Oh, Eden bought them. She got a lot of things—*vêtements* and, ah, stuff." His triumph at remembering a new English expression faded, and he gave her a solemn look.

She was going to kill Caleb—

"Right," Josh said, his smile returning. "Good night. Here she is." He handed the instrument back.

"Yes?" Eden said.

"Thanks for taking care of the clothes," Caleb said. "Josh would have stood out like a sore thumb in sandals and knee socks. I'll have a credit card sent to you on my account. Dad will pay you back for the expenses today."

"There's no hurry," she said stiffly. After all, she thought ruefully, she still had ten or so dollars left in her own account.

Caleb laughed, a rich sound that flowed over her like honey. "Your first day sounded busy. Save some energy for the weekend. We want to take in all the Fourth of July festivities."

Before she could respond to that, he said good-night and hung up. She replaced the phone slowly, her thoughts awhirl. Had he forgotten she'd be leaving on Saturday when he returned?

If he returned, she corrected.

On Tuesday, she and Josh went to the museum. After a quick tour, they joined her mother for lunch at Gino's East.

"There's writing all over the walls," Josh exclaimed when they'd entered and he had a chance to look around.

"And the windows, curtains and light bulbs," Jane added.

"Who did this?" he asked.

"I think the owners invited people to put their names on everything just for the fun of it." Eden wrapped a string of hot cheese around a pizza slice and laid the slice on Josh's plate. She and her mom helped themselves. "Here, put your initials on something if you can find room." She handed him a pen.

"Here's a space," the waitress said, stopping by the table. "Stand up." She steadied Josh while he stood on the bench and wrote *JR* high on the wall. "Neat," she said when he'd finished.

His eyes were shining when he sat down. Eden felt a tug at her heart. It took so little to make a child's day. "You must tell your dad about this next time he calls," she said.

She ignored the fact that her mother was watching her with that approving benevolence parents beam on their children when they're behaving especially well. It entered her mind that Jane might have ideas about her and Caleb.

Would she try again with him? The passion was still there, smoldering away, like a hidden spark waiting for the right moment to explode into flames.

Flames that had burned clear through her, leaving her with an empty feeling inside for months after their aborted engagement, she reminded herself with the ruthlessness she'd accused Caleb of.

For a moment, the empty feeling returned, and depression, dark and heavy, settled over her. Sometimes life could seem so pointless.

Self-pity, she diagnosed, and shrugged it aside. She had no time for indulging useless emotion. During the remainder of the week, Eden and Josh went to the zoo, to the harbor for a cruise on Lake Michigan and to the Children's

Artifact Center, a sort of hands-on museum of archeology that they both enjoyed.

They went to fast-food restaurants for lunch, watched videos in the evening and read *Lassie* at bedtime. Josh was getting a full dose of American culture and picking up vocabulary at a rate just short of amazing.

Caleb called every night and listened patiently while Josh told him all he'd done that day. "You're doing a good job," Caleb told Eden one night.

Her heart went on a roller-coaster ride.

"Tomorrow is the celebration, yes?" Josh asked when he was in bed on Friday night. "The Fourth of July?"

"That's right."

"Are we going to meet my dad at the airport?"

"I hadn't planned on it. We can ask when he calls."

"All *right*." Josh had picked up the inflection perfectly from the hero of a family sitcom they had watched earlier.

While waiting for Caleb to call, Eden finished the book she'd been reading every night. She glanced at the clock. It was almost ten.

They talked for a while. She reminded Josh she would be leaving the next day when Caleb arrived home.

Apprehension formed in his expressive eyes. "Not to return?"

"I'll be here during the day when your father's at work," she quickly explained, sorry that she'd alarmed the child. The one thing he needed now was stability in his life.

"Good," Josh said in evident relief, giving her the megawatt smile guaranteed to break young girls' hearts a few years hence.

The minutes ticked by. Ten o'clock came.

"I think it's time for lights out," she said gently.

He looked at the clock. "I'm not sleepy. Couldn't we stay up for a little longer?"

She couldn't refuse. "Fifteen minutes."

They played riddle-me-ree and took turns trying to guess what "it" was.

The grandfather clock in the entrance hall played the quarter-hour chimes. Eden watched the stoic expression creep over Josh's face, making him look older than his years.

She realized she, too, had been looking forward to the call, but unlike Josh, she hadn't let herself expect it.

That was the worst part of love, she admitted. One grew to expect certain things from the beloved, and then was disappointed when they failed to live up to those expectations, as she had been time and time again many years ago.

Had she expected too much of Caleb during those deliciously insane days they'd been together? She frowned, uncertain.

It didn't matter, anyway. Josh was her worry now.

"Your father most likely had to attend a dinner tonight," she said matter-of-factly. "He wouldn't call after ten. He'd think you were in bed, fast asleep. And so you should be."

When she leaned down to kiss him good-night, Josh put his arms around her neck and gave her a mighty hug, the first outward sign of affection he'd shown her.

Eden experienced a strange sensation as she inhaled his clean, little-boy scent and felt his small, warm body pressed to her breasts. She knew she would miss him terribly when the summer was over. This solemn, lovable little fellow already had a place in her heart. Misty eyed, she turned out the light and crept out of the room.

The night was cool. Josh snuggled against Eden in the patio chair on the upstairs balcony off her bedroom, where the household had gathered to watch the fireworks display. They had a clear view of the lake from this vantage point.

Josh was excited…and worried. "My dad's going to miss it," he said for the fourth time.

"Yes," Eden agreed, keeping the anger out of her voice.

Caleb was supposed to have returned to Chicago on a morning flight. He had called early that morning to inform them.

Her bag had been packed and waiting, ready for her own departure, since breakfast.

"Maybe his plane crashed," Josh said.

Eden smiled down at the earnest face turned up to hers. "Nah, his plane was probably late getting off the ground, or maybe his taxi took a wrong turn and he missed the connection."

"Maybe he is in the traffic jam," Josh said, grinning. He had taken to the expression when she'd used it earlier that week and used it often.

"Maybe."

The fireworks display started with an impressive burst that went from red to white to blue before finishing with an explosion of pinwheels whirling off into the night sky.

The wind cut through her light sweater, and she worried about Josh being warm enough in his jacket and pajamas. "We need a warmer wrap," she said, and prepared to rise.

"Sit still," a deep voice said.

Before she could react, a warm suit coat dropped around her shoulders, enclosing her and Josh in a cocoon of warmth and a pleasant male cologne.

"You made it!" Josh said, excited by his father's arrival as much as by the celebration. "Only one fire-cracker has gone off."

The boy had thought it hilarious that *jam* and *cracker* could refer to something other than food. Eden had discovered he had a dry sense of humor, similar to his father's. She would have to remember to tell Caleb.

She glanced over at the new arrival. He had one hip propped on the railing close to her chair. He spoke to his father, then Henry and the housekeeper before speaking to her.

"Sorry I'm late," he said, looking directly at her. "I cut it too close and missed my flight. I had to take standby on the next one out."

"Josh was worried about you," she told him, letting him know his actions affected other people and that his son was the one who deserved the apology.

In the dim light, she could tell from the set of his lips that her reprimand—which was much kinder than she actually felt—had irritated him. Tough turkey, as Josh would say— another expression he'd picked up from television.

Caleb reached over and ruffled Josh's hair. "Thanks, sport. I'm glad someone was concerned about me."

The boy grinned and turned eagerly back to the display as another starburst of color brightened the sky.

She huddled deeper into the jacket and pulled the lapels around her and Josh. The fireworks continued, punctuated by an occasional exclamation from the child. He decided he would be a "fire shooter" when he grew up.

"I think the fire chief handles it," his grandfather said.

"Then that is what I will be," Josh decided, sounding so much like his dad that Eden had to smile.

"You'll have a business empire to run," Caleb said. "I thought you would take over from me."

Josh looked troubled for a second, then figured it out. "I will do both," he declared.

Two determined males, she thought. They were bound to clash when Josh was older...unless someone was around to keep the peace between them.

Such as yourself?

She shook her head slightly, denying the half-born

wish. It would be a mistake to allow herself to think along those lines.

They were silent for the rest of the fiery display. When it was over, Caleb scooped his sleepy son off Eden's lap and carried him to his room. Eden trailed behind.

"It's late," Caleb said. "Have you had your story hour?"

She shook her head. "The fireworks took its place."

"Would it be okay if I read him a short story?"

Josh sent her a pleading glance.

"Of course," she murmured.

"Is he ready for bed? Teeth brushed and all that?"

"Yes." She watched Caleb settle his son in bed, then choose a Dr. Seuss book from the bookcase. She laid his jacket on a chair. "I need to get on the road—"

"What?" Caleb shot her a frown.

She frowned back at him. Evidently he'd forgotten their agreement. She should have been home hours ago. "Now that you're here, I'm to go home. That was the arrangement."

An impatient expression crossed his face. She noted the worry creep into Josh's eyes as the two most significant adults in his life seemed on the brink of a quarrel.

"It's too late for you to be out on the streets alone. If you'll wait until I finish the story, we'll discuss it."

Not wanting to give Josh cause for alarm, Eden managed a smile and quietly left the room. Before she closed the door, she heard Caleb start on the story. He read with great verve, which made his son laugh.

She tried to picture Caleb as a boy, listening to the silly rhymes and laughing, but she saw him as a man, his eyes dark and passionate when he looked at her....

She fled to her own bedroom. Restless, she paced beside her packed suitcase for a few minutes, then went down to the study to find a book while she waited.

Mrs. O'Leary was there, setting out a tray of sandwiches and drinks. "Caleb is always hungry when he returns," she explained. "He doesn't like airline food." She surveyed Eden's slender figure and shook her head in disapproval. "I thought you might join him. You don't eat enough," she declared before she bustled out of the room.

Eden eyed the food. She *was* hungry. Josh's disappointment and her anger with Caleb had kept her from enjoying dinner. She had a thing or two to say to her employer.

She took a sip of lemonade and settled on one of the matching sofas to wait for Caleb. Leaning her head back, she realized she was tired. She closed her eyes and rested for a moment, not thinking, but letting herself float. Tension drained slowly from her, like a trickle of sand running through an hourglass. She yawned, and yawned again…

A few minutes later, Caleb stopped on the threshold, then crossed the ancient Persian rug and took a seat on the sofa opposite Eden. He settled back and studied her as she slept.

He wondered if this was what marriage to her would have been like—a late-night snack for the two of them while the rest of the household slept…then lifting her into his arms and carrying her up the stairs to their bed. Undressing her…

There was nothing sentimental in his feelings for Eden. He wanted her. That was simple enough. Old-fashioned, natural lust. Nature's way of ensuring the survival of the species.

His cynical thoughts didn't soothe his temper the way they usually did. It irritated him when Eden turned those honey brown eyes on him in accusation.

He'd missed his plane. So what? He'd made it back in time for the fireworks.

What she didn't understand was that he'd worked

damned hard to finish his business in Washington, so he
wouldn't have to return on Monday. What Miss Know-It-
All didn't know was that he planned to take some time off
to be with his son and help him adjust to his new life here.
In fact, if all went well, he intended to work half days for
the following week.

Righteous anger roiled in him. He ought to wake her
up and tell her a few things. He lunged to his feet, side-
stepped the coffee table and bent over her, intending to
shake her awake.

She opened her eyes.

Caleb froze, one hand on her shoulder.

Her eyes were fascinating—the warm brown of tiger
eye gems with golden streaks all through them. The pupils
were wide in the dim light of the study—a beckoning entry
into her soul. He wanted to crawl in and never come out, to
rest there in the warm depths of her love as he once had....

An ache pierced through him, filling him with a need
so strong he couldn't deny it.

Without thinking, he dropped to his knees. Their lips
were on the same plane, and he leaned forward. Her lips
were incredibly soft, the bottom one fuller than the top.
Hunger raged through him.

He gathered her into his arms, bringing her against his
chest, hotly aware of the slender suppleness of her body
as every cell in his recalled her uninhibited response to
his caresses.

"Eden," he groaned, the need intensifying.

Her hands touched him, hesitant, trembling, seeking. He
opened his shirt and let her find his flesh, wanting her to
feel the heat in him. He slid his hands under her cotton
sweater. Fire burned in him.

She turned her mouth away from his. He kissed her face,
everywhere he could reach, starving for the taste of her.

"Caleb, no," she whispered.

"Yes," he said, fierce in his passion. He craved an answer to his desire, the sweetness of her response, once so wildly, so trustingly, given.

"I won't," she said, just as fiercely. But her hands stayed on his chest.

"Touch me," he demanded, "the way you used to."

"This is madness." It was a feeble protest.

He laughed. "Yes, but a heavenly madness." He attacked her ear, the taut cords of her neck. He sought her mouth again.

She gave it to him reluctantly. Triumph filled him. Taking her hand, he rubbed it over his chest, showing her what he wanted. He found her bra. It opened easily. He followed its line around her rib cage and pushed his hands under the material until he cupped her breasts in his palms.

He could feel her heart beating.

"Your heart is like a bird in a cage, frantically beating its wings, wanting to escape," he told her. He shifted slightly and pressed against her, lying on the sofa with her and slipping an arm beneath her head.

He guided his leg between hers until they lay entwined. "I want you. It's been driving me crazy all week, knowing you were here, in my house, and I wasn't."

She made a sound in the back of her throat. A protest, he thought. He wasn't having any of it, not now.

"Say you want me," he ordered softly, savagely.

"No."

"Yes."

She turned her head restlessly from side to side, avoiding his mouth, denying him his reward for all the hours he'd put in that week, trying to get home at the time he'd said, trying to get back to his son...and her.

"No," she said. Eden caught his bottom lip between

her teeth and bit him…not hard, but strong enough that he knew it.

He lifted his head and stared at her. She fought the need to accept the hot promise in his eyes. She wanted his lips on hers. Wanted it desperately!

"You're trembling," he murmured, nuzzling her with his nose, then planting hot, moist kisses along her cheek. "You want me like hell. And that bothers you, doesn't it? Proud, stubborn Eden, who has all the answers."

He taunted her with his words and with the power of his body against hers, inciting the passion she knew she must deny. She moved her head back and forth against his arm.

"I want you, too. It's hell," he confessed, his eyes dark, but glowing from the inferno their passion induced. "I want skin on skin, nothing between. I want my mouth on you, all of you. That shocked you the first time, remember?"

"No," she said, shocked anew that he would remind her of how naively wanton she'd been.

"Where I led, you followed. Willingly. Eagerly."

Because she'd loved him, she silently protested, excusing her weakness.

"You want me now," he concluded. He caressed her breasts with the gentlest of touches.

It would be so easy, she thought, to give herself to him again…to fall in love with him all over again.

The tears collected and slipped from her eyes.

Chapter Six

When the moisture touched his face, Caleb drew back, darkness clouding the passion he felt. He was offended, he found. He wanted her to feel only passion.

"Tears, Eden? For now or for what might have been?" he demanded, as callously as he could past the huskiness in his throat.

She pushed his hands away from her and sat up. "Perhaps for the future that will never be," she told him. There was sadness in her beautiful eyes and in the slight smile she gave him.

He got to his feet. "I'll drive you home."

She shook her head. "I've been taking care of myself for a long time, Caleb. I don't need your help."

"I wonder if you ever needed me," he mocked, but he was half-serious when he said it.

She turned her back to him and arranged her clothing. He had a sudden vision of stripping each piece from her, each new view of her a treasure he'd stored in his heart.

"Why did you ever agree to marry me in the first place?" he asked. She hadn't seemed to care about his money. Of course, that was before she'd lost her own. No, she still didn't seem to give a damn about material wealth.

When she turned to face him, he detected pity in her eyes. He gave her a cutting glance to let her know he didn't need it.

"Caleb," she said softly, on a weary sigh, as if she thought any discussion would be useless.

"You lambast me for breaking my promises, for being late when, in reality, I'm working like a dog trying to finish up and get home. But what about your word to me? You once said you loved me more than life itself. You said you'd marry me. What about *your* promises to *me?*"

Eden pressed her hands together against her middle. He would never forgive her for walking out on him, but she knew only his pride had been hurt, not his heart. Seeing his concern for Josh made that clear.

With her, he'd been impatient, eager only to make love, as if that would make up for all the lonely days since she'd last seen him. It occurred to her that it was the same between them now.

"If you can't see the truth, I can't explain it to you," she finally told him. "You'll have to figure it out for yourself. I hope it isn't too late when you do," she added coldly, then was ashamed of the spite in her tone. "For Josh's sake."

Caleb looked as if he'd like to strangle her. "You always go for a man's weak spot, don't you?" he accused. "My desire for you. My love for my son."

Her heart ached at his words. She wondered if he realized how he separated the two of them in his mind. For her, there was desire. For his son, there was love.

Hearing the truth didn't make it easier to bear. "And your wife, Caleb? What did you feel for her?"

The anger disappeared, and his face became devoid of expression. "The same as she felt for me," he said coldly.

"Your father…" Eden knew she was intruding where she had no right to go. "Your father said you married on the rebound. Both of you."

"He's right." Caleb gave her a smile that chilled her. "I'm consistent in my choice of women, aren't I? I manage to pick the ones who don't give a damn about me."

"That's not true," she protested, stung by his cynical tone. "I loved you—"

"But not enough," he said. "Not enough to stick with me. As for Antoinette, she didn't care at all."

"She—she must have. She had your child." Eden couldn't believe his wife hadn't fallen madly in love with him.

"No," he said harshly. "Once she had Josh, she didn't need a husband in her life. She pushed me away…." He stopped, then frowned angrily. "You always make me say things I regret," he muttered, giving her an accusing glare.

"I'm sorry," she said softly, ashamed of her prying. "Truly sorry, Caleb. Maybe if…" She'd started to say, "if you'd tried harder," but realized it wasn't her place. She'd already delivered her opinion on much of his life. His marriage was definitely off-limits.

He didn't answer, but stared at the floor, lost in some memory from his past, one that hurt. She felt the loneliness in him, like some vast gulf that he couldn't cross.

"I'm going home," she wearily. "I'll be back Monday morning."

Without further argument, she walked out of the room. She collected her luggage, went to her car and started home.

Before she left the drive, another car fell into place behind her. Caleb was escorting her home whether she liked it or not. He stayed with her until she turned into her drive, then he swept on past. He turned around in the driveway next door.

Eden entered her home like a rabbit returning to cover after outwitting a fox—tired, ragged in spirit and worried about the future.

After rain on Sunday, Monday dawned as one of those impossibly beautiful days that beckon to the soul. The sky was a wash of pure blue. The air was clean, the temperature perfect.

When Eden pulled into the drive in front of the Remmick home, she had already planned the week's activities. Now that Josh felt comfortable with her and his new home, she was going to expand his horizons a bit. He needed to meet his peers.

Henry opened the front door and hurried down the steps to take her canvas tote bag before she lifted it from the trunk. "They're in the breakfast room," he told her after they'd greeted one another. "Go right in."

"Thanks." She went down the hall to a tiny, plant-filled room, which had been used for drying herbs and flowers at the turn of the century. She paused at the threshold before entering.

Caleb sat at the table with Josh. They each had a bowl of cereal in front of them.

The boy was still in his pajamas, but Caleb was dressed in a blue suit. He looked like the successful executive he was—wealthy, intelligent, commanding. She felt daunted by the aura of power that emanated from him.

How could she have ever hoped to capture and hold this man of the world?

She hadn't, she reminded herself. He'd returned to that world without giving her a second thought.

"Come in, Eden," Caleb invited, rising and holding a

chair for her. His smile mocked her startled hesitation, while his dark eyes drifted over her at a leisurely pace. "It's a lovely morning, isn't it?"

"Yes, it's gorgeous out today." She took the chair and nodded at the offer of coffee, but declined food. "Good morning, Josh. Did you have a nice weekend?"

"Yes. Dad and I went sailing on the big lake…Lake Michigan, I think." He glanced at his father for confirmation.

"Yes."

"In the rain?" Eden couldn't quite keep the note of concern out of her voice. Storms on the Great Lakes had broken freighters apart like toys. A tiny sloop would be nothing—

"The wind was perfect," Caleb said, as if that explained everything. "I don't think Eden is much of a sailor, Josh. We'll have to take her out and show her how much fun it is."

Josh's eyes lit up. "Today?"

"Another day."

Eden wondered if Caleb realized he had conveyed a promise in the words. Josh would take him literally. She'd have to remind Caleb to keep his word. Which meant they'd have another quarrel.

She lifted her chin, ready to take him on. He had given Josh to her keeping. She'd see that the child wasn't hurt.

"What did you do yesterday?" Josh asked her.

"After my mom and I got back from church and the rain stopped, I painted the front porch while she went to the museum."

"*Bon-papa* allowed me to help him whitewash the shed once," Josh told her solemnly. "I would do this for you."

She was touched. "Why, thank you, Josh, but I'm painting an entire house. It's rather large—"

"Why couldn't he help you?" Caleb broke in. "It would be a good experience for him."

"Well," she began, uncertain what to say.

"What're your plans for today?" he continued.

"I thought Josh and I would swim at the country club. I assume you're still a member?" When he nodded, she smiled at Josh. "Do you swim?"

"*Oui*...yes."

"He's very good," Caleb put in, giving his son a proud smile.

Josh looked at his father with shining eyes, then told Eden, "My dad taught me. Brother Sebastian gave me lessons after that."

Eden wondered what a monk would wear while swimming.

"A bathing suit, the same as anyone else," Caleb said.

Her gaze jerked to him, startled. He was grinning. She had to smile as she realized he'd accurately read her mind.

"Are you coming here for lunch?" Caleb asked, interrupting her rather dazed state.

"Uh, I thought we'd eat at the club, then check out the afternoon programs to see if there's anything we like."

"I'll join you at lunch," he said. He rose and, picking up his dishes and napkin, took them to the kitchen. When he returned, he gave Josh a kiss on the cheek, then paused by her chair.

Eden tensed like a rabbit ready to flee. He wouldn't dare give her a kiss....

"See you later," he said. One eyebrow lifted slightly in a wicked challenge, while a matching grin tilted the corners of his mouth. He'd known exactly what she'd thought!

A little of the morning's brightness seemed to fade after he left for his office. She refused to let herself think of him in the skyscraper where they'd made eager, desperate love so very long ago.

"Eden?" Josh laid a hand on her arm.

She brought herself back to the present. He had finished his cereal. "Come. Let's take your dishes to the kitchen so Mrs. O'Leary won't have to worry about them."

At ten, they went to the country club next door to swim and meet some of the children who, she hoped, would become Josh's friends and playmates. Eden was relieved to see several young people who were students from the academy.

"See that blond girl over there?" She pointed out the girl to Josh. "She's in my honors French class. I think that's her younger sister with her. We'll say hello when we get a chance."

"Do you think they will like me?" he asked, while they paused inside the gate and looked over the area.

Her heart went out to him. For all his maturity, he was still a child, one who hadn't had much exposure to other children. It was a stroke of luck to run into Chris, who was outgoing and friendly.

"Sure. You're a very likable person." Eden spotted a table next to Chris's. "Come on."

They crossed the patio in front of the wide picture windows that separated the restaurant from the less formal dining terrace, where waiters were setting up umbrellas over white tables.

Eden glanced self-consciously at her bathing suit. It was new, a one-piece in bright red with high-cut legs and a ruffle over the bust. She wondered if the ruffle made her breasts look fuller than they were.

Caleb had never seen her in a swimsuit, she recalled. It had been too cold for swimming when they'd met. Of course, he'd seen her in nothing at all. Heat seared along her veins as a picture of him, all virile, masculine strength, leaped into her mind.

Caleb, on his knees before her, caressing her as if she were a goddess. Caleb, bringing her hand to his chest, needing her touch like a man coming in from the desert. Caleb, pressing his heart against hers, listening to their joint, frantic beats....

"Eden?" Josh was looking at her curiously.

"I'm sorry. What did you say?"

"This table?"

"Uh, yes, this is fine." She put the brightly striped canvas tote on one of the chairs and kicked off her thongs. She supervised putting on sunscreen. "Ready to go in?"

"*Oui*...yes."

Side by side, they took the plunge. As Caleb had said, Josh was an excellent swimmer. And Eden was long out of practice, she found, panting when they reached the other end of the Olympic-size pool. Josh was hardly winded.

"Race you back," he challenged, his eyes alight with mischief.

Eden groaned. "You swim as fast as a shark," she protested. "I think you ought to let me have a head start."

"But no," he protested. "I'm just a kid."

Another line he'd picked up from a TV sitcom. Eden grinned. He was fast becoming Americanized. Best of all, he was coming out of his shell and learning to joke.

"Okay, but if I lose, I'm going to sulk," she warned.

Without further ado, she pushed his bangs down over his eyes and took off, but at a leisurely pace. He caught up, then passed her, his boyish, thin arms slicing through the water with little splashing.

"Say, you're really good." Chris ambled over and spoke to Josh when they'd climbed out and sat panting on the side of the pool, their legs dangling in the water. "Hi, Miss Sommers. Who's this awesome swimmer you've got with you?"

"Josh Remmick. This is Chris Worth, one of my best students last year." Eden was pleased to make the introductions. "Josh is from Martinique. He's going to be living in Chicago from now on. I'm helping him get acquainted."

"Super. You on the Olympic team?" she asked Josh half-seriously.

Josh glanced from her to Eden, not quite sure of this type of humor. Eden smiled but remained silent, encouraging him to speak for himself.

"Uh, *non*...no."

"Well, great. We could sure use you on the club team here. One of our best swimmers in the sunfish category moved away last week. Would you be interested in trying out?"

Eden nodded when he looked at her.

"I would like that, yes," Josh said with grave sincerity. "Thank you."

"Like, wow." Chris giggled and tossed her mane of strawberry blond hair behind her shoulder. "You're cute. Let me call Kathy. You would be on her team. I'm the assistant coach. Hey, Kath. Come 'ere." She motioned to her younger sister.

Josh turned red, but his eyes were filled with admiration. Eden recognized a bad case of puppy love at first sight.

"Whoever loved, loved not at first sight?" The line from *Romeo and Juliet* haunted Eden during the rest of the morning while the young people became acquainted. As soon as Kathy saw Josh swim, she wanted him on her team.

"Boy, we can sure use you," the five-year-old said, her voice sounding just like a professional swimming coach.

Josh, often formally correct, even strutted a bit at having two females—one of them an *older* girl—praise his ability. When the younger set got up a game of Marco Polo, Eden brought out a French novel and began reading in the shade of an umbrella.

"Bonjour, mademoiselle," a husky voice murmured close to her ear. *"Cette livre, est-il intéressant?"*

Eden, unaware of Caleb's approach, blushed as hotly as Josh did each time Chris praised him. "It's okay." She put the novel in the tote and gazed helplessly at Caleb, while he seated himself next to her.

He, too, was dressed casually, in swim trunks and a shirt. The shirt was fine white cotton with embroidery down the front, the kind often used as formal wear in the tropics. He was tanned and unbearably handsome, his body lithe and fit. She looked away as something hard and painful formed inside her.

Glancing around the terrace, Eden saw several admiring glances being tossed his way. He smiled and waved to a couple of women he knew.

"I see Josh has found some playmates," he commented.

"Yes." She told him about Chris and Kathy and the swim team.

Caleb studied her in an introspective manner while she talked. She wondered what he was thinking.

"I hope to have a birthday party for him next month at the pool at your house. If he joins the team, he'll know lots of kids by then. It will sort of consolidate his position with the group."

"You're doing a good job," he said when she stopped. "My father was right to insist on hiring you."

Eden felt puffed up with pride. Like Josh, she thought. How we long for a word of praise from those we love…or admire. She didn't love Caleb. That would be foolish. But there were things about him to admire.

"Speaking of jobs, you don't look like you're going back to work today." She ended with a question in her voice.

"I told you I was going to take half days off."

"Yes, but I didn't really think you—" She stopped abruptly, but it was too late.

His smile segued into a frown, but it was thoughtful rather than angry. "Did I break my word to you so often, Eden, that you'll never believe anything I say in the future?"

She risked a quick glance at him. His face was serious. For a second, she thought she saw sorrow in his eyes.

The scene blurred as she looked away. She wouldn't let him make her feel like this again—all bothered and breathless, all confused and full of longing. She mustn't.

"It doesn't matter what I believe. Josh thinks you can do no wrong. His feelings are the ones that count."

To her surprise, Caleb didn't get angry over her reminder of his duty to his child. "I know," he agreed softly, watching his son learn racing turns at the end of the pool, with Chris and Kathy shouting instructions. "I hope I do better by him."

Than you did with me? she wanted to ask, but didn't. The past was done. Let it lie, she advised herself sternly. Don't feel sorry for him…or yourself. They had made their choices long ago.

She sighed as the heaviness weighed on her spirit again. She wasn't unhappy, but life seemed more difficult all at once.

"Are you ready for lunch?" he asked.

She nodded.

"I'll call Josh. Shall I invite the young ladies to join us?"

"That would be nice."

He reached for her hand and pulled her to her feet. "I can be nice at times," he murmured seductively, giving her a sideways glance, then a grin.

Her heart thumped like mad in her chest. She slipped

on a short robe and waited while he spoke to the children, then preceded him when he indicated she was to do so. She was aware of his eyes on her back while the waiter showed them to a table on the terrace.

In a few minutes, Josh and the two girls joined them. Josh introduced his friends to his dad. Eden noted the way the boy's eyes lingered on the teenager. Then she saw Kathy's gaze on Josh. Oh-oh.

"A triangle in the making?" Caleb joked to her as the other three were occupied with food choices.

"I think so. You've become very perceptive of late," she responded. Although, she admitted, he used to read her like a book. Up to a point.

"I'm trying," was all he said. He looked at her intently.

She couldn't figure out if he was trying to tell her something personally, or only assuring her of his sincerity toward his son. The latter, she decided. She shouldn't take anything between her and Caleb personally. He felt only desire for her…and that wasn't enough…had never been enough.

At the end of the meal, Caleb and the children decided on sundaes for dessert. "We'll have to walk around the lake here to burn off all those calories," Caleb said to Josh when the huge concoctions arrived.

"Then will we cook the hamburgers outdoors, like you said yesterday?" Josh asked.

"Tonight, yes. A cookout. You and I will be the chefs."

"Like a shoot-out." Josh giggled, delighted with the idea.

"Well, maybe not that dangerous," his father said with a laugh. "Although I am pretty wicked with a spatula." He looked at Eden, their eyes meeting in mutual recall.

Once, when he grilled steaks at her house for her and her mother, they had kissed, and the steaks had caught on fire and nearly burned to a crisp before they noticed them again. Her mother had commented it was a good thing the steaks had been small or else the fire department might have come. Eden had been embarrassed, but Caleb had only laughed.

Laughter from a nearby table broke the moment. Eden drew a deep breath and felt the heaviness close in on her. She didn't know why she felt so dismal. She tried to shake off the mood and listen to the conversation.

"Where will you go to school this fall?" Kathy asked Josh.

"I don't know." He looked at Eden for guidance.

"I don't know, either. Have you picked out a place?" she asked Caleb.

"I was going to discuss it with you."

"There's a super school near here. That's where I go. Josh can go there, too. We can come over and practice for the swim team in the morning before school starts. Your mom and my mom can take turns driving us." Kathy had it all figured out.

Eden quickly checked to see if Josh was upset by this mention of mothers, but he took it in good grace.

"My mother is dead," he said solemnly, "but Eden can bring me. Would you?" he asked, anxious to gain her approval.

"This fall? I'll be in school myself. Perhaps Henry can drive you over. You'll have to ask your father."

It was clear the idea of asking his dad hadn't occurred to Josh until then. Eden realized she'd had to suggest he ask Caleb's permission about things several times. Apparently the absentee father had left the decisions up to his in-laws in Martinique. That needed to change. Caleb should be the primary authority in the child's life. She'd explain that to him when they were alone.

"I'm sure we can arrange something," he told Josh, bringing a smile to his son's face.

During the meal, she noticed that Caleb mostly listened to the young people discussing school and other activities. There was a slight frown on his face, as if he were thinking hard and deep about something important to him.

A business deal, Eden decided cynically. What else occupied his every waking thought?

"Would you like a bite?" Caleb inquired politely.

Before she could refuse, he expertly fed her a spoonful of ice cream smothered in hot fudge and whipped cream. It was cool and delicious against her tongue. She gulped it down and licked the sweetness off her lips. Caleb watched her, his eyes slitted to dangerous levels.

He signed the bill and they rose to leave, after promising to meet the girls tomorrow for more practice. Chris and Kathy were determined on Josh making the team.

"They are nice, are they not?" he asked as they walked back to the house by skirting the edge of the golf course.

"Yes. Girls are very, very nice," Caleb said. "Except when they're not." He gave Eden an enigmatic grin when she looked at him.

"Until they're provoked into anger by males," she corrected.

Josh dashed ahead to look for stray golf balls in the rough.

"Sometimes," Caleb suggested, his dark eyes on his son, "they can be provoked to emotions other than anger." He swung the tote bag lazily between them.

She swallowed as she remembered the passion he had induced in her. So effortlessly, she admitted. She had been so easy for him to seduce. Was he thinking along those lines…that she might take care of his son during the day and him at night?

Never!

She walked faster, needing to get away from him and the unsettling effect he had on her.

At the house, Caleb supervised his son's shower, while Eden went to her room and showered, too; then she changed into white shorts and a red top with white polka dots. She tied her hair back with a red scarf and went to check on Josh.

He was sitting in an easy chair with his father. Caleb was reading an adventure story about a baby elephant. She drifted on down to the study, then out onto the back patio. Mrs. O'Leary brought out a pitcher of ice tea and one of lemonade, along with a plate of cookies. Eden smiled her thanks and poured a glass of tea. She sipped the cold liquid, hoping it would soothe the tightness in her throat.

For some reason, she felt like crying. It was the strangest thing. Her emotions zigzagged on a course of their own choosing these days, it seemed.

After a while, Caleb came out. "Josh is napping."

She nodded and continued to gaze at the trees along the edge of the property. "What's that out there?" she asked.

He looked toward the woods. "An old gazebo. Shall we go explore it?"

She shook her head. "Not now. Maybe when Josh wakes."

"Scared?" It was a direct challenge.

"Yes."

He heaved a deep breath, then poured a glass of tea for himself. "I'm surprised that you admitted it."

"Admitted what?"

"That the attraction is still there. And the hunger. The need." He paced restlessly to the edge of the patio and turned. "I didn't expect it to be this strong, though. Did you?"

She shook her head. "I thought I could handle it. That first day when you interviewed me…I thought that, if you offered me the job, I'd take it and the past wouldn't matter."

He gave a snort of laughter. "The past doesn't. It's the present that's tearing me apart. At the pool, I looked at you…in that red bathing suit…. I didn't think I could handle it at all there for a moment."

"Caleb," she said in protest, as yearning rose within her.

"I'm not going to fall for you again," he told her with harsh determination.

Her pride came to her rescue. "No one asked you to."

He nodded. "Just so we understand each other."

When he walked off, she felt like throwing something at his arrogant head, but caution intervened.

Mr. Remmick came out of the study and joined her. "A stubborn man, my son," he said. "He needs you."

"Mr. Remmick, please don't set your hopes on something that can never be," she advised as gently as she could.

"Three lonely men," he continued, musing aloud. "We all need you. Save us from our lonely selves," he requested simply.

He smiled kindly at her while she stared at him in helpless confusion, not sure how to answer. After a moment, she smiled back, realizing he must be joking with her.

She watched Caleb stroll down to the woods and disappear into the octagonal gazebo. She thought of the redhead he'd brought to lunch that day. If he was lonely, it was of his own making.

Chapter Seven

"See ya next week," Kathy called.

"Right," Josh yelled out the window as his friend ran up the steps to her house.

Eden waited until Josh rolled the window up before taking off. He'd made the country club swim team and was fully immersed in its activities. Kathy's mother had driven the kids to practice each morning that week, and Eden had picked them up.

Caleb was out of town.

She mused on his absence and its impact on his son. As soon as Caleb had left last Sunday, Josh had stopped mentioning his father. It was as if the man ceased to exist when he went away on business trips. That troubled her.

Josh had yet to give his trust to his father, although they'd had a companionable month together. Well, she didn't really expect the child to wipe out five years of neglect—yes, Caleb, *neglect*, she argued with his image in her mind—in a single month, she reminded herself.

Ah, but it had been a wonderful month. Hiking, sailing—which she'd discovered could be relaxing or exciting, according to how one did it—and swimming, both at the club and at the house.

"Do you know what tomorrow is, Josh?"

He considered carefully. It was an endearing trait, but sad, too. He rarely tossed off a careless answer, but mulled over each question before he replied. He had learned to be cautious with his words and his trust.

As we all do sooner or later, she reminded her own troubled heart. It wasn't Caleb's absence, but his presence that had made her more and more cautious this past month.

"Saturday," Josh finally said.

"That's correct. Saturday *and* the first day of August."

He gave her a curious glance, uncertain of the significance of the date.

"Your birthday is August twenty-first. That's only three weeks from now, you know." She gave him a quick glance and a smile before taking off with the flow of traffic when the light turned green. "I thought we'd have a birthday party. What do you think?"

His dark eyes, so like his father's, lit up. The megawatt smile flashed on. "Like, wow!" he mimicked Chris, who was hooked on old TV sitcoms and movies at present.

"We could invite your swim team over for a swimming party and a cookout at the pool."

"My dad and I can do the cooking," he exclaimed. His smile disappeared as he reconsidered. "If he can make it."

He will, she silently vowed. Or else.

As she turned into her drive, she remembered all the times she'd waited for him, watching anxiously from her bedroom window for his lights in the drive. And then the phone call would come.

"Eden? Caleb," he would say in his quick, hurried

manner. "Look, something's come up, and I won't be able to make it over this evening…."

Or this week or this month, she recalled, the memories going bitter as the old hurt resurfaced, just as wounding now as it had been way back then.

Tears blurred her eyes as she watched Josh scramble eagerly from the car and head for the porch. Perhaps he was the wise one. He'd learned not to let himself care too deeply about Caleb. He wouldn't let himself depend on a man who might or might not appear.

With a sigh, she climbed out and joined Josh on the porch. He had already pried the lid off his can of paint and was busily stirring until it was smooth.

During her odd moments off that month, she'd painted the porch and steps with marine paint. During the past week, she'd finished the porch ceiling and walls. Now she and Josh were doing the trim around the windows and the shutters.

"I'm ready," he announced.

"Then I'd better get cracking." She removed the shutter he'd painted yesterday from the sawhorses and laid another across them. "You'll need to wipe it off in case any dust has settled on it since we washed them Monday."

"I remember," he told her, indignant that she'd reminded him.

"I'll go in and change to my work clothes." She dashed inside and up the stairs to her room. She changed to old cutoffs that had an interesting pattern of paint smears, and an equally besplattered shirt.

The sound of a car horn drew her to the window while she finished buttoning her top. She saw Caleb step out of his luxury sedan and wave to his son. Her heart did a nosedive.

Like her, he was dressed in cutoff jeans and a T-shirt whose printed message had long faded to obscurity. The sun cast sparkles of light over his black hair. In spite of his sailing and swimming, there were no blond streaks through the thick waves.

She had loved to run her fingers through the smooth strands, to cup his head in her palms and kiss him slowly and thoroughly all over his face. He had liked it, too.

Holding very still, he would close his eyes and let her caress and tease him in any way she wanted. He'd been content with that for long, blissful intervals. Until the hunger grew too great.

She sat down on the window seat when he walked up the front steps and disappeared from view. The heaviness that had come over her at odd moments all month pressed on her spirit.

Caleb had done very well by Josh so far. But then, anybody could be attentive for a month. During their time together, he'd called or flown in to see her every spare minute at the beginning. She'd hardly been able to study because all her spare time had been his.

It had been that way the second month...and the third....

But then his time with her had lessened. The press of work, he'd said. At first, she'd teased him about his "management-by-crisis" style. By the time of their engagement party, it had no longer been funny.

She wondered how her mother had put up with her father's long hours of work. Of course, he hadn't had to travel the way Caleb did. He had come home every night after a ten- or twelve- or sixteen-hour day.

Her mother had used her time in charitable pursuits and bridge games with her friends. That life didn't appeal to Eden. Maybe she expected too much, but she wasn't willing to compromise.

Love had to come first...before business, before money,

before everything. Maybe that was unrealistic, but she wanted to be a part of her husband's life. She wanted to share dreams, to raise a family, to grow old together. All of those things took time.

Time that Caleb had never had, she reminded herself. Because he hadn't chosen to make it available.

She pushed the oppressive unhappiness away and went down the steps and out onto the porch. Both males were busy with paint and brushes. Josh had a huge grin on his face.

"Look, Dad is helping," he said proudly when she reappeared.

Looking into his young, eager face, she managed a smile, but she turned a wary gaze on Caleb.

"Good afternoon, Eden. I hope you don't mind if I join in. I missed you guys…" He glanced at his son and back to her, causing a frisson to run down her spine. "So I cut today's meeting short and took an earlier flight home. My father told me of your activities."

His voice rippled along her taut nerves. It was fluid and melodious, with a caressing warmth. She'd always loved his voice. He paused and lifted the paintbrush from the trim, clearly expecting an answer from her.

"No," she said. "No, of course we don't mind." She pasted on a teasing grin. "An extra hand with the work is always welcome and appreciated. Now, if we could get my mom to do her share…"

Josh snickered as she let her voice trail off. It was a standing joke—that Jane always found something she just had to do when it came time to wield a paintbrush. Josh, on the other hand, couldn't decide if he wanted to be a fireman, a painter or, like his father, a businessman who flew all over the world making important decisions.

"Dad, did you have to fight a warlord?" Josh asked as he drew a strip of paint along a shutter.

Eden had asked Mr. Remmick to explain Caleb's work, so Josh would understand why his father had to travel so much. It had been a good lesson. Eden had pointed out all the places on the globe where spices, tea and coffee were grown, while Mr. Remmick told of the problems of dealing with governments, cartels and such.

Caleb grinned. "Your grandfather must have been telling you tall tales while I was gone."

"He told me about the time the mean guy was going to hold you for…" Josh looked at Eden. "A kind of money."

"Ransom?" she suggested, appalled at this news.

"Yeah," Josh exclaimed, his eyes wide.

Caleb exchanged a glance with Eden.

"What happened?" she asked. "I didn't hear this story."

"A punk bought into the coffee cartel I was dealing with. He decided to flex some muscle and demanded double the contract price. When I refused and walked out, he had me…detained." Caleb shrugged, as if it had been of little consequence.

"When?" she asked. "When did that happen?"

"The week before the party."

She knew he meant their engagement party.

He looked directly into her eyes. "The other cartel members wasted no time in applying pressure in the right places. I was released, the deal went through as planned and no harm was done. I had to spend the rest of the week with the State Department boys, giving them an overview of the situation when I returned to the States. That's why I was late."

"Why didn't you tell me—"

"You didn't give me a chance," he cut in.

"You called every night that week. You could have told me what was happening and why you had to be in Washington."

"I didn't want to worry you."

She shook her head and picked up a spare brush. After pouring paint into a plastic bowl, she started on the window trim next to Caleb. "Or maybe I wasn't important enough in your life to be told you'd been abducted and held for ransom."

"Dammit, Eden—" He broke off after a quick glance at his son's face. Josh was looking anxiously from one to the other.

"It doesn't matter now," Eden said on a quieter note.

"No," Caleb agreed. "It doesn't, not now."

They were almost finished with the trim when Jane came home from work. "My, that's looking really nice," she said, pausing on the steps after saying hello to everyone. "Such good work deserves a reward. How does fried chicken sound?"

"Mmm, my favorite," Caleb approved. "How about some barbecued beans and coleslaw to go with it?"

"No problem," Jane assured him. "Josh, how many drumsticks can you eat in one sitting?"

"Drumsticks?" He turned to Eden, puzzled.

"Another word for chicken legs," she explained. "Legs were my preference when I was your age. I always ate two of them."

"Two, please," he told Jane with a grin.

"We'll make ice cream for dessert," Jane decided. "Have you ever turned the crank of an ice-cream maker?"

Josh shook his head, fascinated by this question.

"Well, finish up and come to the out-kitchen so we can get started on it. We'll do that first. Then, while it sets, I'll cook dinner."

"Go ahead, Josh. I'll clean the brushes when I'm through," Eden volunteered.

When Josh and her mother went into the house, Eden turned back to the last edge of the windowsill. Caleb, she noted, had finished the trim on the window he was doing.

He moved two steps closer to her. "I used to be a leg man myself," he murmured with a wicked gleam in his eyes, "but later I decided breasts were better."

She gave him a repressive glare, while heat churned inside her. "How interesting," she said coolly.

"Yes, funny how your tastes change when you get older." He moved away and sloshed his and Josh's brushes into a container of water to clean the bristles. "Sometimes a man finds the things he once thought were vital are not so important after all."

She completed the section and stepped back to check her work, as if looking for missed spots. She used the time to think. When she turned, she found him watching her with an expression in his eyes that she couldn't read.

"Yes," she said slowly, aware of undercurrents between them. "Life can do that to a person." She hesitated. "Caleb, if you'd told me…the kidnapping…it would have made a difference."

"Why?" he asked, his face subtly altering.

"Don't," she said, angry with him.

"What?"

"Don't close me out. You always did that. You made me feel like a child there at the end. You taught me passion and longing, the physical part of being a woman, but you shut me out from all the rest—the problems, the dangers, even the triumphs. As if I were too simple-minded to understand."

"I never thought that of you." He studied her, as if trying to fathom her thoughts.

She shook her head and dropped her paintbrush into a can of water. Wiping her hands on a rag, she tried to hold back, but the words tumbled out unbidden. "That night…if only…"

"If only you'd been willing to listen?" he suggested, the anger rising in him again. "But you weren't. You withdrew into your ice castle and no one could touch you, not even me. Especially not me," he finished bitterly.

The truth of this hit her in the heart. Yes, she'd refused to listen, but it wasn't all her fault. "It was too late by then. Don't you see? I no longer felt I had a place in your life. I thought you were tired of me, that you were pulling away."

"Well, I can certainly relate to that," he said.

Eden remembered that his wife had pushed him away, out of her life and apparently out of their son's life, too.

She suddenly wanted to hold him…and to be held by him. As if their mutual misery could act as a shield to protect them from the bad things of the world. When she spoke, her voice was husky.

"We can learn from our past mistakes. That's one of the nice things about being human. We can do things differently in the future," she said, and wondered if he'd think she was asking for another chance. "I'd better go in. Mom might need some help."

"I'll be along when I finish these." He indicated the brushes. "I brought some other clothes. Okay if Josh and I shower and change before eating?"

"Of course."

She quickly went inside, heading down the broad hall to the family-style kitchen with the big oak table next to the windows. She found her mother and Josh stirring the ice-cream mixture.

"I'm going to take a shower, then I'll be down to help," she said, interrupting their pleasant chatter. "Josh, your dad brought clean clothes for the two of you. You can use the upstairs bath like you did yesterday. Show your father where the towels are when he comes in, okay?"

"Right. Thank you," he added, remembering his manners.

Eden proceeded to her room. She quickly stripped off

her clothes and stepped into her bathroom. In a few minutes, she emerged, feeling clean and refreshed by the shower. Her heart beat fast at the thought of Caleb doing the same a few paces down the hall from her.

She wondered how it felt to take a shower with a man. Books mentioned it frequently. It sounded romantic… sexy, too.

Closing her eyes, she thought of how his hands would feel, gliding all over her with the silky smoothness of the lather between them. The breath hissed between her teeth as she turned from the fantasy and pulled on slacks and a yellow top.

With hands that trembled slightly, she put on makeup, combed and dried her hair, then tugged on sandals. She owed Caleb an apology for her earlier remarks. He probably had thought he was protecting her by not sharing the fact that he'd been in danger. Men were like that. They never thought of simply telling their loved ones the truth.

Loved one? Had he truly loved her?

She left her room, afraid to search for an answer to that question. It was coming too close to what she wanted *now*.

Stopping in the kitchen doorway, she watched Caleb and Josh turning the crank on an old-fashioned ice-cream freezer in the out-kitchen, a porch that had been enclosed. Her mother stood with her back to the door, busy at the stove.

Eden listened to the male voices, one a baritone, the other a childish treble that would deepen with puberty into his father's range. Two handsome males—intelligent, desirable, lovable…so very, very lovable….

She gripped the doorjamb, knowing what her heart was telling her. No, she thought desperately. She couldn't be so foolish. She wouldn't fall in love with Caleb again. No. No. *No*.

Biting her lower lip, she tried to keep her emotions under control. She managed to regain her composure, but the effort took all her concentration. When she glanced up, she found Caleb watching her.

His gaze held hers as he looked directly into her eyes. For a second, she saw understanding there and the same tormenting ache she felt, the same yearning. He let her delve deeply into his soul. He was letting her see inside him…

"Is it about done, Dad? This handle is getting hard to turn."

The moment passed as Josh asked about the ice cream. Caleb took the handle and turned it. "I'll take it now," he said, his voice husky. "Another five minutes should do it."

Eden hurried into the kitchen and began setting the table for the four of them. Then she sliced peaches, sprinkled them with a little sugar and lemon juice to keep the slices from turning dark and placed them in the refrigerator for dessert.

The meal was a pleasant one. Jane kept them smiling with stories about people who came to the museum. "One man said he and his wife had seen an ancient body at another museum, one that had two heads buried with it," she told them. "His wife asked their tour director why there were two skulls with one body. The docent told them the smaller one was the pharaoh's when he was a child, the larger one when he was a man."

"Quick thinking," Caleb said. He and Eden burst into laughter.

"What's funny?" Josh demanded.

"A person has only one skull for life." Caleb rapped gently on his son's head with his knuckles. "It grows with you."

"Oh. So he couldn't have had two heads." He spoke so solemnly that it drew another laugh.

"Not normally," Caleb agreed. He leaned back in his

chair with a satisfied smile. "That was one of the best meals I've ever had. Don't tell Mrs. O'Leary I said that," he advised his son. "We wouldn't want to hurt her feelings, but her fried chicken doesn't stand up to Jane's."

"Oh, go on with your blarney," Jane said modestly, but her smile was pleased. "It's so pleasant outside this evening. Let's have dessert on the porch, shall we?"

She shooed them from the kitchen and insisted on cleaning up by herself when Eden and Caleb offered their help. When Josh said he would help, she sighed and said she couldn't refuse.

Eden went out onto the porch, Caleb right behind her. He settled into the swing. "Come on," he invited. "I'll swing you."

She started to refuse, then saw the challenge in his dark gaze. He expected her to reject his offer. Lifting her chin, she went over and sat on the other end of the swing, a respectable two feet between them. He set it in motion.

A sigh escaped her.

"Tired?"

"Yes," she said.

He looked around the porch. "You did a good job. Your talents never cease to amaze me."

She frowned slightly and glanced at his expression to see if he was being facetious. He looked sincere. "Thank you." She sighed again. "Now, if I had the rest of the house done…"

"It's a big job, all right. If you'd take the full salary you were hired at—"

"I'm not staying with Josh twenty-four hours a day," she cut in. She came home at night when Caleb was at home.

He heaved a sigh, plainly exasperated with her stiff pride. "It would be easier on your mother if you took the money and hired someone to do the painting for you," he told her.

Eden knew Jane didn't like painting but felt guilty if she

didn't help. With the money Caleb was willing to pay, they could afford to hire someone to finish the rest of the house.

"I'll be in and out a lot for the next few weeks," he went on. "I'd like you to be there for Josh. Will you?"

His intent regard flustered her. "I…well, if you really need me—"

"I do," he interrupted. "We do. All of us. My father has missed you this past week. He says you haven't been staying at the house."

"He misses beating me at chess at night after Josh is in bed," she scoffed. But it was nice…being missed.

"Why haven't you been staying?"

She sat very still. He swung them back and forth, back and forth, very gently. "You were supposed to be back Tuesday. I saw no need to stay one night. Besides, Josh has swimming every morning now. There's nothing to do. You'd be paying me for sitting and reading. The arrangement with Kathy's mother allows me to get some of my own work done."

"I'd feel better if you were there. Henry's main duty is to my father. I don't want him worrying about anything else. You said you'd take the job. Are you going to do it or not?"

She whipped around and glared at him. "If I'm not doing it to your satisfaction, find someone else."

"Oh, you are," he drawled. "Josh loves you. My father thinks you walk on water. Henry and Mrs. O'Leary fall all over themselves to make you happy. What kind of spell do you cast, that everyone wants only to please you?"

"Really, Caleb—"

"We all cringe if we draw the slightest frown from you. But if you smile…ah, but if you smile, then the world is bright once more, and we're caught up yet again in the magic you weave."

His voice dropped to an intimate whisper that seemed to caress each and every nerve in her tense body. She sank slowly into a reverie that was strangely peaceful, yet filled with the sweetest ache of longing.

She didn't move as he came closer to her, his eyes devouring her with the intensity of the hunger she saw in those dark, turbulent depths. He paused a few inches from her mouth.

The sweet ache turned to a pure, heartfelt yearning for completion in his arms. She wanted his lips…now!

"Eden," he murmured. Lifting one hand, he cupped her face and touched her lips with his thumb, then slowly, slowly brushed back and forth across them, his eyes watching every nuance of expression in her eyes.

She closed her eyes. It wasn't her own magic that caught her. It was his. His voice. His gaze. His touch.

The swing stopped moving. He shifted. Then she felt his thigh against hers. His hand left her face, slipped down her neck and behind one shoulder. He pulled her to him.

If he'd been hasty or rough, she might have had a chance to resist. But he was gentle, so very gentle. Each touch asked permission for the next. Spellbound, she waited.

And then his mouth touched hers.

She couldn't prevent the gasp that escaped her throat, nor the tiny shudder of desire that trembled through her. She knew he heard her, that he felt the betraying shiver. He didn't alter his course, but continued until her breasts were against him. She felt him take a deep breath, then the kiss began in earnest.

He pressed closer, harder, with a controlled desperation driving him. His muscles rippled under her fingers, reminding her of how strong he was.

One hand moved to her face again, his long fingers delving into her hair and holding her head still while he traversed every inch of her face, tasting her like a starving man.

"Caleb," she said, a feeble attempt at protest.

He took her hand and held it against his pounding chest. "This is what you do to me. Only you. From the first. Why? Dammit, why?"

Caleb sought and found her lips again, driven by the demons of his passion for this woman. The woman who had walked out on him, he reminded himself. After letting him into paradise, she'd coldly turned him out because he'd been late.

"Kiss me," he demanded.

Her mouth opened in a small gasp when he bit on her lower lip.

"Yes, like that. Open for me. Kiss me back this time. Eden, Eden." He heard his own voice as if from a distance, speaking low, almost in a chant.

He slid his tongue into the moist sweetness of her mouth, and his body went into total, shocking arousal, harder, faster than it had ever happened to him…except with her. Always with her.

He pushed her away and stood up, pacing to the end of the gazebo and staring out at the sunset. The flare of color across the sky matched his soul—fiery reds, molten golds, brooding shades of lavender shadowing into purple, then indigo.

And beyond indigo…the black silence of deep space. Where his soul had been for seven years. Life was easier that way, he'd found. Why bring it back for a summer fling?

"Dad?"

He whirled around. Josh stood in the shadows behind the screen door. "Yeah, Son?" he managed, sounding close to normal, as close as he could get with his blood swirling through him like a spring tide at the flood.

"I brought the spoons and peaches. Could you open the door?"

"Sure."

Josh came out onto the porch and carefully set the items, along with a handful of napkins, on the table between the Adirondack chairs. "Jane's bringing the ice cream. She let me spoon it up."

A knot formed in Caleb's throat. What simple things it took to please the young. He glanced at Eden, sitting there in the deepening twilight, as remote as a goddess.

She had a way of closing herself off when she wanted to. Like the night of their broken engagement. He frowned as a kaleidoscope of thoughts ran through his head. Eden closed herself off when emotions went too deep, he realized. When she was hurt beyond words, she simply folded in on herself. Like now.

Had his kiss bothered her that much? A small flurry of excitement raced through him. Before he had time to analyze it, Jane appeared, bearing a tray. He took it from her and placed it on the low table.

"I made some chocolate sauce, too. That was your favorite, wasn't it, Caleb?"

"Yes," he said, his gaze on Eden. "Thank you, Jane. You're a very thoughtful person."

The mood became jolly as they indulged themselves in the icy treat. Josh liked both chocolate sauce and peaches on his. Caleb preferred just the sauce. Jane and Eden took only the fruit, he noticed. Eden talked very little, but, as usual, her mother carried the conversation. He wondered why he'd never noticed that Eden was a rather reclusive person compared to her mother.

There suddenly seemed a world of things to learn about her, things he'd never noticed during that wildly passionate first encounter. For instance, he'd never imagined her with a paintbrush in her hand, or a saw. He glanced around the porch and noted the signs of her handiwork.

"This is really good," Josh told Jane.

"Don't eat too fast, or you might get a headache," Eden advised. "I used to do that. The cold freezes the throat or something. It's the oddest hurting sensation."

Caleb smiled, yet he felt a sadness inside. She had a way with children—another thing he hadn't known. She talked to Josh as a friend, yet when she needed to assert authority, she did it without sounding angry. He wondered what other things he hadn't noticed during their hectic courtship.

Twilight turned to dusk. He rose. "Josh and I had better hit the road. I thought we'd get up about five and see if we couldn't catch some fish while they're hungry. Maybe you ladies would like to join us for dinner? Mrs. O'Leary has a great recipe for fish."

"That would be lovely," Jane said with a smile.

He turned to Eden. Her hesitation bothered him. Once, she'd followed his lead without question, her trust in him absolute. How had he lost that trust? he wondered.

The silence grew awkward before she finally nodded.

"Fine," he said. "Around seven, then. Good night."

Giving Josh a tug to get him on his feet, Caleb led the way to the car. They were silent almost all the way to the house.

"That was fun, wasn't it, Dad?" Josh asked.

"Yes, it was."

There was another stretch of silence.

"I, umm, saw you and Eden…."

Caleb sighed and took the bull by the horns, so to speak. "You saw me kiss her?"

"Uh-huh." Josh fidgeted with his seat belt strap. "You like her, don't you?"

Caleb hoped this wasn't going to be the birds-and-bees talk. He wasn't up to it. "Yeah, I like her."

"I do, too."

"Umm," he said. "Look, you can see the moon on

the lake from here," he pointed out, hoping distraction would work.

"Yeah," Josh said. "Dad?"

Caleb sighed internally. "Yes, Son?"

"You *really* like Eden?"

He was at a loss for an answer. "She's very nice."

"When you kissed her…does that mean… I mean, is she going to be my mother?" he blurted.

The question stunned Caleb. He hadn't realized Josh would put that interpretation on events. He glanced at his son as they turned into the drive to their house. The boy's expression was anxious, yet there was such hope in his eyes.

Caleb swallowed hard as emotion hit him. It was evident what Josh wanted. He would have to tell his son the truth—that there was no chance of marriage between him and Eden. But not tonight. He was too damned tired to talk. When he got back from his trip…

"Would you like that?" he asked. He cleared his throat of the huskiness that had lodged there.

Josh fidgeted some more. Then, "Yeah, I guess," he mumbled offhandedly the way males did when something meant a lot to them.

Caleb stifled a groan. How the hell did life become so complicated? he wondered. And what was he going to tell his son?

Chapter Eight

Eden leaned her head back on the comfortable chair and idly listened to her mother and Mr. Remmick talk. They were in the study of the Remmick home, having after-dinner drinks and coffee. Caleb wasn't in the room. He was reading a story to Josh.

As promised, the fish dinner had been delicious. Mrs. O'Leary had seasoned the bass perfectly with Cajun spices and had served it with a mouth-watering sauce.

"You're absolutely right about the changes in today's society," Jane agreed, in response to a statement Mr. Remmick had made.

Eden noticed how pretty and animated her mother looked. She and Mr. Remmick had found a host of common interests. Caleb's father was a perfect host—attentive and charming.

"I noticed it in last Sunday's wedding announcements," Jane continued. "Used to be, an announcement would tell the groom's occupation, then add something like, 'After a honeymoon in Hawaii, Mr. and Mrs. Smith will reside at Oakmont.' Now it says, 'Mr. Smith is an attorney with the so-and-so firm. Dr. Smith will begin her career as a medical researcher at Johns Hopkins,' or 'Mrs. Harper-Smith will complete her Ph.D. at Northwestern.'"

"Women don't want to be wives anymore," Mr. Remmick mused.

"Oh, love and hormones are as strong as ever," Jane assured him. "But with the divorce rate sky-high and women being left to care for the children on their own in numbers never before seen in history, it's only good sense to prepare for a career."

"But who will raise the children?" he asked.

"Well, it should be a joint responsibility."

A movement at the door caught Eden's eye. Caleb stood there. He was listening to the conversation. His gaze flicked from his father to Jane while she spoke, then it came to rest on Eden.

A tumult of longing swept over Eden. She picked up her cup and took a drink of coffee in order to hide her feelings.

"Josh would like to tell you good-night," he said to her.

"Oh. Of course." She composed herself and rose.

"Tell him again that the fish he caught was delicious," Jane said.

"I will." Eden went out of the room, aware of Caleb in the doorway as she moved past without touching him.

She hurried up the stairs and into Josh's room. He was tucked into his bed. Only the night-light was on. She sat beside him, delivered Jane's message and added more praise of her own. When she bent forward, he wrapped his arms around her and hugged her as tightly as he could. She gave him a kiss on the cheek, touched at his show of emotion, and held him close.

"Dad really likes you," he whispered. "So do I. I'd like you for a mom…for my mom."

A lump came into her throat. "Josh," she began, seeking words to let him down gently.

"You could live here all the time then. You like it here, don't you?" He pulled away and gave her an anxious look.

"Of course. This is a wonderful home—and you'd be a wonderful son. But marriage involves more than that. Your father and I…it's just that…it can never be," she finished, her words sounding lame to her own ears.

"You kissed him," Josh reminded her, with the inexorable logic of a child. "At your house last night."

She closed her eyes for a second and wondered how she'd gotten into this mess, why she hadn't seen it coming. She knew Josh loved and trusted her, but she hadn't suspected his thoughts lay in this direction.

"Doesn't that mean you like him, too?"

"Of course I like him—"

"I asked him if you were going to be my mother."

"Oh, Josh," she murmured helplessly. It wasn't right to question a child about a conversation with his parent, she reminded herself, stilling the longing that rose in her.

"He asked me if I'd like you for my mom, and I told him I would," Josh continued eagerly. "You'll be my mom when you and Dad marry, right?"

Dear heaven, what was she going to tell this wonderful child who'd just laid his heart bare before her? Tears blocked her throat.

"You should never ask a woman about the state of her heart, Son," a strong, masculine voice drawled behind her. "It isn't done in polite society."

She whirled around. Caleb leaned against the doorjamb. From the guarded perusal he gave her, she knew he'd heard the whole conversation. Heat rose in her face as he crossed the room, the half smile that always grabbed her heart on his lips.

"People kiss for a lot of reasons. It doesn't necessarily mean a commitment between them. Friends kiss when they haven't seen each other in a long time. You and I kiss good-night. So do you and Eden. Sometimes people kiss because they're excited about something else, and it has nothing to do with the other person."

Josh looked at Eden for confirmation.

"Yes," she managed to say. "That's right. It doesn't have to mean anything special."

He looked so disappointed, it tore at her heart. She smiled, pulled the sheet to his neck and kissed him again. Caleb turned the light out and closed the door after they went out. They walked down the hall in silence.

At the steps, she stopped and faced him. "Why didn't you tell him the truth right off the bat?" she demanded.

"What truth?" he asked, his face going hard.

She returned his glare. "Why, that there's nothing between us. And never will be."

"Nothing?"

His hand snaked out and grasped her behind the neck. "Nothing?" he repeated.

With his superior strength, he drew her to him until their lips were only a breath apart.

"Nothing?" His eyes bored into hers, demanding a retraction of her rash statement.

"Nothing that matters," she whispered.

He released her so suddenly, her head jerked back and lightly banged the wall behind her.

"Are you okay?" he asked, a flicker of concern in his gaze.

She nodded.

He took a deep breath and let it out in a loud sigh. "How

do things get so complicated?" he muttered, more to himself than her.

"They don't if we don't let them." She moved down one step. "I'd appreciate it if you would tell Josh the truth right off instead of answering a question with a question. You were always good at that, deflecting my anger with a question and never telling me the truth."

"Is that what I did?" His tone was sardonic.

"Yes. When I'd ask why you were late, you'd laugh and ask if I had missed you, or if I'd believe you if you told me. It made me so furious, as if you thought I weren't capable of understanding the truth. Don't do that to your son, Caleb. It's better to state the facts than to mislead a person with false hope."

"Did I give you false hope?"

She turned and looked at him without speaking.

Comprehension dawned. "I'm doing it again, aren't I?"

Eden rolled her eyes and didn't answer.

He laughed. "Perhaps you'd better coach me in how to talk to people," he suggested.

"It isn't my concern," she informed him, starting down the steps. "Except as it affects Josh and my relationship with him."

"He likes you," Caleb said softly. "He *really* likes you."

"I like him, too," she admitted, ignoring the taunting light in Caleb's eyes. She paused when they reached the downstairs hallway. "He's a fine person, Caleb. You should be proud."

A pensive expression came over him. "Sometimes I wonder what I did to deserve him."

"Children are a gift, not a reward," she said firmly.

"Like love, Eden?"

The silence hummed between them. She couldn't move. She couldn't answer without giving away emotions she refused to let him see. His gaze probed hers, as if looking for an answer in her soul.

After what seemed to be an eternity, she turned and hurried into the study, where her mother awaited her.

"Ready to go home?" she asked a shade too brightly.

Jane immediately stood. "Yes. I have to work tomorrow afternoon at the museum. We have three student tours coming in."

Caleb spoke to Eden. "You'll stay at the house next week while I'm gone?"

She nodded. "I'll bring my things when I come over Monday."

"Good," Mr. Remmick said heartily. "You should come, too," he said to Jane. "You and your daughter liven up this mausoleum."

Jane laughed and thanked him, but declined. They said their farewells. Caleb walked the two women out to their car.

"Drive carefully," he said, leaning down so he could peer in the window at Eden.

"Yes, I will." She quickly started the engine and drove off, leaving him standing in the dark drive.

"Such a pleasant evening. Caleb's father is charming." Jane laughed softly. "Like father, like son, like grandson. That could be a formidable threesome if they all decided they wanted something and went after it together."

Eden caught her mother's thoughtful glance. "Not me," she protested without thinking.

"I'd say John and Josh very much want you as part of the family." Jane paused, then added, "From the way Caleb looks at you, I'd say he wants you, too."

Eden tightened her grip on the steering wheel. "No," she managed to choke out past the knot in her throat.

"What do you want, Eden?" her mother queried gently.

"I think you're in a position to have all your heart desires…if you'd just reach out and take it."

Eden's thoughts and emotions went into a whirlwind of confusion. What did she want?

Simple. To be loved.

No, it was more complex than that. She wanted a place in her husband's life. She wanted to know that he would consider her and their family first, and that he'd try his hardest to be with them. She didn't want to be taken for granted—the little wife who waited patiently at home for her mate to have time for her in his busy schedule.

Was that so unreasonable?

She sighed, disheartened by the longing that was growing in her daily. She couldn't seem to control it. When Caleb touched her, she melted. That was a fact she had to face.

Everything she'd ever felt for him had returned, stronger than before. Everything. Including her love.

Caleb felt as if his smile were frozen on his face. He took a sip of the drink he'd nursed for over an hour, then grimaced. The truth was, he was bored. More than that, he was lonely.

There. He'd admitted it. He was lonely for his son.

And for Eden?

His body immediately went on alert at the thought of her. He walked over to the open door and onto the lanai. The moon cast a shimmering path to the far horizon.

The stairway to heaven, Eden had once told him. That had been another time, another place. This was now. And he was an advisor to the United States representative at the Pacific Rim tariff-and-trade negotiations here in Tahiti.

During the day, he was busy listening to the haggling at the official meeting, then discussing strategy in private.

It was the evenings that bothered him. An endless round of cocktail parties was not his idea of a great time.

A picture of Eden and Jane in the kitchen, of him and Josh turning the handle of the ice-cream freezer, leaped into his mind.

Yeah, that had been fun.

He sighed and pressed his thumb and finger to the bridge of his nose. A headache pounded behind his eyes.

Setting the cocktail glass on a table, he walked down the steps and out onto the sand of the beach. A group of palm trees lined the edge of the resort property. From the shadows, he heard a soft giggle, then noticed a couple.

They were wrapped in a tight embrace, the woman leaning against the trunk of a palm while the man kissed her face eagerly, blazing a path to her mouth.

Caleb could remember doing the same with Eden. A tumult of feelings pierced him. He'd never gotten over her, he realized.

He'd thought he felt only anger and scorn for her, the woman who had ditched him at their engagement party without a backward glance, but he hadn't. The old hunger had resurfaced the moment he saw her again.

Farther down the beach, the land curved in a half circle. The path ended in a tumble of rocks. He climbed up and sat on the top boulder and watched the restless ebb and flow of the sea.

He felt the same inside—pulled this way and that by forces he could no longer ignore. A man would be a fool to fall for the same woman who'd walked out on him, he reminded himself ruthlessly.

The past flashed into his mind—the scene in the hospital, where he'd held his wife. Sweet, gentle Antoinette, whose final moments had been filled with concern for him and for the child they'd had together.

Antoinette's dying wish was that he try again with the woman he'd once loved. "Josh needs a mother, Caleb. Promise…promise me this…a mother for our child." She'd clung to him with surprising strength until he'd agreed.

Then she'd gone to sleep, and he'd sat there on the bed, holding her frail hand and regretting all the times he hadn't been with her, all the things he'd never said to her. They'd lived separate lives—hers steeped in motherhood, his in business. They'd made their choices, but…was that any way to have a marriage?

Caleb sucked in a deep breath and forced the memories to retreat. That time was past, he reminded himself.

But his promise to Antoinette throbbed in his head.

No, dammit, he wasn't going to lose himself in Eden again. He knew better. However, there was Josh to consider. His son was the important thing in his life.

Suddenly he knew what he would do. A smile briefly settled on his mouth as he thought of Eden's reaction.

Henry greeted her as soon as she opened the car door on Monday. "You're to call Caleb's office right away," he said. He removed her suitcase from the trunk. "The number is on the desk in the study."

Her first reaction was fear. Caleb had been hurt—a car wreck, a kidnapping. Silly. He was probably going to tell her he would be gone for the month and couldn't make it for Josh's birthday. She'd kill him, she decided quite calmly.

Henry took her overnight case from her in the hall and went up the stairs to her room. She entered the study. It was empty.

On the desk pad was a note with a number on it. She dialed. The secretary answered on the first ring. Eden introduced herself.

"Oh, yes. Caleb wants to know if you and Josh can

join him in Tahiti. The meeting is going to go over into next week—"

"What?" Eden said blankly.

"The international tariff meeting scheduled for this week has been extended, making it go over into next week—"

"Caleb wants me and Josh to—to fly out there?"

"Yes. He says he'll have the weekend free." The secretary's voice dropped to intimate levels. "I think he's lonely for his son. He told me to help with the birthday party. If you'll give me a list, I'll send out the invitations and arrange for the caterers, the cake and all that."

"Uh, Mrs. O'Leary is making everything. I've already arranged for a clown show. There's only the invitations to go out…." Eden's voice trailed off. Her mind was in a whirl.

"Great. I'll take care of those. Now, I've checked flights and booked your seats. The tickets will be waiting for you at the airline ticket counter. You leave in the morning at seven. It's a long flight, so be sure to take some books and games. Ask Henry to bring me the list of names, okay?"

"I will."

"Have a good trip."

"Thank you. Bye."

Eden hung up in a daze. Tahiti? He wanted them to come to Tahiti? She couldn't believe it. There were a thousand things to do. First, Josh had to be informed. And she'd have to check with Chris regarding his swim-team commitments.

"Josh," she called, running up the stairs. "I've got some news for you."

Their itinerary took Eden and Josh from Chicago to Los Angeles to Hawaii to Tahiti, with two changes of planes. Josh, she found, was an excellent traveler. He exercised in his seat by flexing his arms and legs and pushing one set of muscles against another.

"Press your knees together real hard," he told her, insisting that she do the exercises, too. "Dad said it was important to keep your legs from swelling."

They played guessing games and tic-tac-toe, then read to while away the time. At last they arrived. Eden blinked in the bright sunlight and looked around.

She didn't see Caleb. It would be just like him to send for them, then be too busy to come for them himself. He'd probably sent a taxi or something—

"There's Dad!" Josh yelled. "Over there. Hey, Dad!"

She looked where Josh was pointing. Sure enough, there stood her nemesis, breathtakingly handsome in white shorts and a blue polo shirt, a white cap shading his face from the sun. He smiled and waved.

They made it through the gate without delay. Caleb grabbed his son, gave him a toss into the air, then bussed him on the cheek. When he glanced at Eden, she drew back slightly.

His expression hardened, and his smile became reserved. "So, you've arrived."

"Yes." She couldn't think of anything to say.

He took their two larger suitcases, gave Josh her canvas tote bag and led the way to the car. When Eden was seated—in the back, at her insistence—she pushed a stray lock of hair from her face and realized her fingers were trembling.

She gazed out the window at the exotic landscape and tried not to notice the fresh, soap-and-shampoo fragrance from Caleb. His hair was damp, indicating he'd showered just before coming to meet them. His familiar cologne stirred old longings in her.

For a moment, a fantasy took hold of her. They were

married. Josh was their son. Caleb had sent for them because he was lonely…for both of them.

Not her, she reminded herself. Caleb loved Josh, not her.

"Here it is," Caleb said, breaking into her runaway thoughts.

The resort was lovely. The main building gleamed white in the dazzling sun. The ocean rolled in on a white beach.

She'd read that there were black beaches of volcanic sand on the island, too. She'd take Josh on a tour tomorrow to see them.

"We have our own place," Caleb said. He drove through a grove of extremely tall palm trees and stopped by a charming cottage set in a group of smaller palms.

"The ocean," Josh pointed out. "We can go swimming."

"Right," Caleb agreed. "There're two pools on the grounds, one saltwater, the other fresh. Also golf, tennis and hiking." He looked over his shoulder at her. "What do you think?"

"It's…it all looks wonderful."

He got out of the car and opened her door before going to the trunk and retrieving the bags. Eden climbed out on shaky legs. She hadn't thought about sharing a cabin in a palm grove with Caleb. Of course, Josh would be there.

The earlier fantasy lingered in her mind as Caleb showed them inside. There was a living room facing the ocean and a modern kitchen, two bedrooms and two baths. If they were married, they would share the large one with the queen-size bed.

"Josh can sleep with me," he said. "We'll put you in here."

"Fine," Eden answered. Her room was done in shades of flamingo pink and white, the other in sea green with touches of the pink.

"Are you tired?" Caleb asked. "You can nap—"

"Let's go swimming!" Josh broke in.

"Your manners need a bit of polishing," his father told him.

Josh was immediately abashed. "I'm sorry, sir."

Caleb tousled his hair. "That's okay, but watch it."

The boy was at once happy again. "Right. Uh, are we gonna go swimming?"

"Yes." Caleb smiled at Eden. "Are you going to join us?"

"In a minute. I want to hang up some things." And get her imagination under control again, she added to herself. "Be sure that Josh has plenty of sunscreen on."

"Yes, ma'am." Caleb gave her a slow grin, then followed Josh into the master bedroom.

After the two males changed and raced off toward the beach, she unpacked and hung up her clothes, then went to do the same for Josh. The heady scent of Caleb's toiletries surrounded her as she put Josh's toothbrush in the bathroom. A tremor ran through her.

These intense reactions wouldn't do at all. She had to be cool and in control if she was going to last out the week without making a fool of herself. Caleb would probably laugh if he could see into her mind…and her heart.

She quickly hung up Josh's clothes and put his other things in the empty drawers she found in the dresser. Seeing Caleb's underwear and extra swim trunks in one drawer made her presence in his bedroom seem much too intimate. She finished and left.

In her room, she undressed and pulled on the red bathing suit. Over it, she wore a red-and-white-striped terry robe. After washing her face and slathering on sunscreen, she put on sunglasses and a wide-brimmed hat and headed out.

"Eden, come on in. This is fun," Josh called as soon as she appeared. She hesitated, then slipped off the robe and ran lightly across the hot sand into the soothing embrace of the sea.

"Welcome," Caleb said. Then he splashed her in the face.

"Why, you," she spluttered, wiping saltwater out of her eyes. At his challenging grin, she struck at a wave and sent a sheet of water in a rainbow arc.

Caleb laughed and dived under the surface, while Josh shouted, delighted with the horseplay. Eden splashed him and started a water fight that lasted until all three were breathless from dodging and trying to get even. When they tired, they left the sea to walk along the shore and look for shells.

Eden wished she had put her robe on. She was acutely aware of Caleb's masculine presence. He was aware of her, too. Every time she glanced his way, their eyes collided.

It was utterly ridiculous…like school kids with a crush on each other. But Caleb wasn't a boy, and she wasn't a young girl. They knew the feel of each other, the trembling response of being body to body while they kissed. The hunger and then the joining….

She forced her eyes to stay on the beach or the sea. With suitable words, she admired Josh's finds. She listened quietly as Caleb explained about anemones and other sea life. Josh found a live starfish and decided to make a wish on it.

His dark eyes, so like his father's, darted from his father to Eden. With a solemn expression, he closed his eyes and made his wish; then he tossed the creature back into the waves.

One look at Caleb's remote expression told her he'd guessed what his son wished for, too. His hard gaze told her it was never to be. He'd never forgive her for walking out on him.

There were two sides to that sword. She would never marry a man who put everything before her and their family. She'd end up hating him, and she'd always wonder why their love wasn't enough to hold him.

She sighed as the heaviness she'd fought for weeks descended on her again. Didn't a person ever get over that first wild-but-sweet, totally tempestuous love?

The answer seemed to well up from some deep, mysterious place inside her, a place that only Caleb had discovered, a place that only he occupied, no other. No, she'd never gotten over him.

"A penny for them," Caleb offered.

She lifted her head and gazed at him. They were alone. Josh had run ahead and was climbing an outcrop of rocks.

"My thoughts?" she asked. She wasn't going to discuss her ill-fated love with him. "I was wondering why you sent for us."

"I was lonely."

She stared at him, then shook her head. "I can't believe I heard that. The tycoon admits he has needs like other humans." Her heart speeded up.

Instead of becoming angry, he smiled. It only affirmed what he'd said. He did look lonely. It was a disturbing insight.

"I thought I'd been pretty open about my needs with you," he murmured. "Seven years ago…and recently, too."

"Desire doesn't count," she protested. "Men can look at a statue and feel that."

"What about women?" He reached out and found the pulse in her neck. "When you look at me, what do you feel?"

She pushed his hand away before he felt the heat that swept through her at his touch. His mood was unpredictable. A dangerous gleam had appeared in his eyes, and he seemed set on taunting her.

"Not anything I can't control," she informed him coolly.

He studied her for a minute more before nodding toward

the rocks and his son. "Race you," he challenged, and started off.

After a startled second, she ran after him. He let her catch up, and together they scrambled up the tumbled boulders and joined Josh, to watch the sky change to the colors of sunset.

"Don't you want to come?" Josh asked. He gave her a disgruntled frown.

Eden shook her head firmly. "I get seasick on fishing boats. Besides, fish hate me. They'd stay a hundred miles away. You and your father will do much better without me along."

Caleb stood behind his son, his dark eyes thoughtful as he gazed at her. She was settled on a chaise longue on the lanai of the cottage, a book in her hand. She waved them off, then watched as they walked along the beach to the boat dock in front of the main resort building.

"Don't forget the sunscreen," she called before they were out of hearing. Caleb saluted, while Josh laughed.

She smiled, lazy and content with the way things were going. Today was Sunday, the last day before Caleb would be caught up in all-day business meetings again. On Tuesday, she and Josh would head back to Chicago.

She wanted Josh to have his father to himself one time. Deep-sea fishing on a charter boat sounded like the ideal "guy thing" for father-son bonding.

In truth, she needed some distance from Caleb. From Josh, too. The boy wanted her to do everything with them. He was looking at the three of them as a family. She needed to ease that notion from his mind. In a month, when school started, she would fade out of his life. Busy with his new friends, he would forget her.

Tears burned her eyes. She blinked and took several deep

breaths. No use mooning over what wasn't to be. She'd once cried buckets over Caleb. It had made no difference.

Laying the book on the patio, she gazed at the waves crashing in to shore. A lovely girl walked by, bare breasted, as many of them went on the beach. It no longer startled her.

Nor did it make her uncomfortable, she realized.

Josh hadn't commented at all on it. Apparently he was used to nudity at the beach. Caleb rarely seemed to notice. When he did—there was one young woman so beautiful even the women stared—he would immediately look at her, and his eyes would tell her how desirable she was.

A tremor washed over her with the restlessness of the churning sea. One more month. If she could just get through one more month.

The men were late getting back. Eden had ordered three seafood salads from room service. She set these and tall glasses of tart fruit punch out for dinner while the guys showered and changed clothes. She removed a hot loaf of bread from the oven; then she heard them talking in the bedroom.

In a minute, they came into the room, fresh but tired looking. She surveyed them. "You don't look too much worse for wear. And neither of you is sunburned. Good."

"Thank you, Mother Goose," Caleb intoned solemnly.

Josh hid a giggle behind his hand. He was freer about showing his emotions now, she thought with a tinge of pride, but he would probably always be a somewhat-reserved person. Like his father.

She listened while Josh told her about the fish that had gotten away—two big ones—and the ones that hadn't, which were too small to keep or not good for eating.

After the meal, Caleb read to Josh.

Eden went out on the lanai. Soft music filtered through

the balmy night from the main cabana, where a combo played and couples danced in the sultry air. The resort attracted a rather young clientele, who gathered every night to dance and chat and flirt.

Mating rituals, Eden mused. So strong. Overpowering, really. That's what had brought her and Caleb together. She could see that now. Their outlooks on life were too different for them to ever have made a couple, but the attraction had been too forceful for them to ignore.

And so they'd both been hurt.

That was another insight. Caleb wasn't hard and unfeeling, caring nothing for anything but his wheeling and dealing. She'd hurt him when she'd broken off the engagement. His love for Josh and for his father were evident.

When Josh fell asleep, Caleb lifted the child and carried him to bed. Then he came outside and joined her in the moonlight.

Without speaking, he held out his hand. She took it. They danced to the distant music, caught in the magic of the moment, unable or unwilling to fight the spell.

She gazed into Caleb's eyes as they moved to and fro, their movements echoing the restless sea. They danced more and more slowly, until they stopped.

He took his hand from her waist and touched her cheek, his caress light, warm, gentle....

He bent his head and kissed her.

Chapter Nine

"Please see that your seat belts are securely fastened."

Eden clicked her seat belt closed and made sure Josh's was tight across his hips. She could still feel the pressure of Caleb's unexpected kiss at the gate. A goodbye kiss. They'd shared so many of them.

For a moment she thought of how it had once been to be young and in love. That first wild, impetuous rapture...

She'd felt that way Sunday night when Caleb had kissed her. While their lips were urgent upon each other, while their hearts had beat in unison, she'd let herself pretend that a moment could last forever and that a kiss was the pledge of a lifetime.

After they had drawn apart, each shaken, Caleb had spoken first. "Things will be different in the future, Eden. You were right. A person has to set priorities. Being with Josh this week, seeing how happy he was..."

Caleb had stopped and swallowed hard. Eden had been moved by the depth of his love for his son.

"Josh needs a family. I want to be part of it. I want him to come to me with his problems."

"I hope you mean that," she'd answered cautiously.

He had released her and stepped away, his eyes on her dark and brooding. "I do."

She wondered now at the intensity of that vow. He'd spoken so fiercely, as if he needed to convince her. But she wasn't the important one in this scenario. Josh was.

Caleb had gained the boy's trust. If he let him down, Josh would turn to someone else. It was that simple. She'd tried to explain that to Caleb, but he'd become impatient with her little homily.

"I'll be there for him," he'd declared with grim determination, and he'd walked off down the beach, his hands in his pockets, tension in the set of his shoulders.

"Here we go," Josh said, breaking into her troubled thoughts.

The plane left Tahiti, banked over the ocean and climbed steadily above the thin cloud layer. Several hours later, they arrived in Chicago. The week in paradise was officially over.

Henry met them at the airport. Mr. Remmick was with him, waiting in the car. Josh kissed his grandfather on each cheek, a rather cosmopolitan manner of greeting. Someday the boy would be a heartbreaker, Eden acknowledged with an outpouring of pride in her heart.

On the ride to the house, Josh snuggled against her and went to sleep. She smoothed his unruly hair from his face. It was going to be hard, very hard, to leave him, come September and the start of school.

Glancing up, she saw Caleb's father gazing at her, a look of compassion in his eyes. She looked away, not wanting him to see into her soul and discover her love and her loneliness.

"When will my son be home?" Mr. Remmick asked in a low tone.

"Saturday."

He frowned. "That's cutting it close. The arrangements for the birthday party are all made. Everyone called and accepted."

"Good," she said with a smile, glad for Josh's sake.

For the rest of the week, she and Josh were busy getting back into the swim of things, as it were. He had a swim meet Saturday morning. Since he and Caleb had swum every day in Tahiti, Josh wasn't out of practice. Chris was pleased. He blushed at her praise.

The swim team acquitted itself well on Saturday morning. Eden smiled at Josh on the way home. He was unhappy about losing.

"No one told us they were going to have a porpoise on the other team," she finally said, hoping to relieve his gloom. "That kid could really churn the water."

Josh nodded and sighed. "I wanted a ribbon to show my dad."

"You have the red one," she reminded him.

"But not the blue."

"There'll be another day." Slim comfort, but that was all she had. When she turned into the drive of the Remmick house, her body went into overdrive. Electricity hummed along her nerves. Caleb should have arrived an hour ago.

He hadn't.

Mr. Remmick explained. "Caleb was requested to stay for the private talks with Japan on trade policies. It was something he couldn't refuse."

Eden nodded in understanding. She knew he was bored with the drawn-out negotiations. He'd told her a little about them each night while sitting on the lanai after Josh was in bed.

It wasn't until she caught a glimpse of Josh's face that she realized the consequences. The child showed no emotion. He took his shower, his manner subdued the rest of the day.

That night, when he went to bed, she realized he had gone through the rest of the day without mentioning Caleb once.

Eden stayed beside him on the bed after they finished their story. She smoothed the lock of sun-lightened hair from his forehead, then felt his face. "You feel a little warm. Are you all right?" she asked.

He shrugged. "I guess."

"You know," she said carefully, "when I was a kid, my father worked all the time. He was almost never home."

Josh didn't look at her. "Yeah?"

"Umm-hmm. It used to make me so mad."

He stared out the window at the night, but she could tell he was listening intently.

"Sometimes I wanted to hit him."

Josh ducked his head. She saw him clench his hands.

"Yes," she went on, "I used to wish that I'd get big and he'd get little so I could hit him." She picked up a pillow, doubled her fist and gave it a blow.

Josh's eyes widened as he glanced at her.

"Do you ever feel that way?" she asked. "Like hitting something until all the anger is gone?" She struck the pillow again, then again.

"Yes," he said.

"Then hit the pillow," she invited. "Go on. It's okay to let the anger out this way. Everybody has angry feelings, especially when a person you love disappoints you."

He hit the pillow tentatively, then a little harder. He whapped it a third time, then a fourth. He paused and looked at Eden. She smiled at him. He blinked, then grinned.

"Better?" she asked.

He nodded. Then he threw his arms around her and hugged her hard. Taken by surprise, Eden hugged him back, then held him as he clung to her until he went to sleep.

She needed to tell Caleb that his chances with his son were running out. Perhaps it would be better if he didn't say when he would be home. Then Josh wouldn't get his hopes up, only to have them dashed yet again. The child had a lot of love to give, but he wouldn't give it to his father much longer.

Sighing, she slipped out of the room and went to the study. Mr. Remmick was there. She enjoyed their quiet talks.

"You're good for the boy," he said. "I'm glad you and Caleb are together again."

She was speechless. Recovering, she hastened to correct his mistake. "We aren't. Not really," she added defensively at his sharp glance. She suspected he knew of the kiss she and Caleb had shared on the swing at her house. "It's a temporary arrangement. Until Josh goes to school."

"I don't like these wishy-washy relationships you young people get into nowadays. If you love each other enough to live together, you should get married."

"We're not living together. I was hired as a tutor and to help Josh adjust to life here. That's what I'm doing."

A long silence stretched between them.

"When Caleb lost you, a part of him died. He was a changed man after that," Mr. Remmick said. He sounded sad, regretful.

"He doesn't seem different to me. Although he says he's trying to change things," she added, to be fair.

"Believe him. We've had several long talks recently. My son wants to raise his children himself. We're changing our methods in the business. No reason the division managers can't handle their own contracts."

Eden's heart leaped to her throat. She thought of having a child, a girl to complete the ideal family foursome. She shook her head slightly, shaking off the fantasy.

"I hope Caleb does change," she said. "Josh needs him."

"What about you? Do you need him?"

She met his perusal with a steady look. "I love him, but I gave up any plans for our future seven years ago."

Mr. Remmick leaned forward and took one of her hands in his. "Don't give up on my son. He needs you. Help him find a new life, Eden, before it's too late for him and the boy. Growing old alone is a lonely thing."

Emotion threatened to overcome her as she realized the hard truth behind this statement. Like her father, Mr. Remmick had ignored his family. Now he paid the price of that neglect. He didn't want his son to make the same mistake.

"Long ago," he said, releasing her and settling back into his chair, "I wanted to achieve great wealth. I wanted to show my father—a hard, bitter man who felt trapped by life—that I could be somebody. I had one driving ambition—to succeed. I did. But the price…no one warned me of the price. My wife stuck with me, but when she was ill with cancer, she told me I hadn't been with her in life, so I needn't stay with her while she died."

Pity rose in Eden. "I'm sorry."

"Yes," he said. There was a wealth of regret in the word.

Henry came to the door. Mr. Remmick stood and, leaning upon his cane, walked out of the study and down the hall to his empty room. His slow, painful steps echoed along the hallway.

In a few minutes, she went to her room and prepared for bed.

The week passed. Although Caleb called every night, Eden noticed a difference in Josh. His conversations with his father were brief. At other times, he seemed listless, and inclined to quiet play with his toy trucks and cars. She tried not to appear overly concerned, but she was worried about him.

She reminded him of his birthday party coming up on Friday. He perked up a bit when she let him pick out the party favors and games. On Friday, they decorated the patio around the pool for the grand event. Mrs. O'Leary made a huge cake shaped like a fire truck, surprising both Josh and Eden.

Caleb called from San Francisco. A heavy fog had descended on the California coast. His plane was grounded.

"Rent a car and drive to Reno or L.A.," she told him.

Caleb didn't respond to her flippant advice. "I'm working on it. Tell Josh I'll be there as soon as I can."

"Right," she said coolly, remembering all the times he'd told her the same thing. Anger burned in her. She suspected she wasn't being fair, but she really was worried about Josh.

"What's wrong?" Caleb asked, evidently sensing her anxiety.

"Nothing. It's Josh. I don't know." She sounded almost incoherent.

"Tell me," Caleb ordered.

"He's quiet," she explained. "Almost listless. I've taken his temperature. He doesn't have a fever, but…" She couldn't put it into words.

There was silence on the line, then, "I'll get there today if I have to hijack a plane," he promised grimly. There was another pause. "Take care, Eden." He hung up.

She went out to the patio, where the birthday party was just getting started. Josh was flushed with excitement as he showed Kathy the cake and refreshments.

"We're making real ice cream," he said proudly. "In a freezer and everything."

Making ice cream was a bigger hit than the clown show. Some of the kids had no idea what went into ice cream. They were fascinated and delighted when they got to take turns at the crank.

Eden smiled her thanks at Jane, who had suggested the treat, and had taken off early to come over and help.

"Children have a great capacity to learn new things," Jane commented as they cleaned up afterwards. "It's a shame we don't make better use of it."

"I agree." Eden sat back and sighed.

The party had been a success, and Josh seemed happy. He was playing at the edge of the pool with a new toy. A surprise had arrived from Caleb—a bright blue bike with racing tires and training wheels. Josh had been pleased with the gift.

But, Eden had acknowledged, he hadn't said a word about his father the whole time, even after she'd explained the cause of the delay. They'd heard no more from Caleb after the call. She was a little worried about him. He'd sounded so desperately determined to get home when he'd hung up.

Later that night, long after everyone else in the house had gone to sleep, she lay in bed, her worry increasing. The evening news had reported that most of California was enshrouded in fog. The San Francisco airport had been socked in for seventeen hours. Some people were trying to charter private planes to take them to other airports.

That would be like Caleb. He'd risk his life getting there.

A sound disturbed her. Sobbing. She threw back the covers and dashed into Josh's bedroom. He was sitting up in bed, sobs shaking his body.

"What is it, love?" She lifted him into her arms and sat in a chair.

"I don't feel good."

"Do you hurt anywhere?"

"I don't know," he mumbled, snuggling against her. His eyelids drooped sleepily. "I just feel sick."

She touched his forehead with her lips, but couldn't tell if he had a fever. Maybe he'd just had a bad dream. Rocking back and forth, she held him for a long time, loving the knobby feel of him—all elbows and knees and sharp bones, so typical of children.

Emotion rose in her, and she was unable to hold it in. "I love you," she whispered.

"I love you, too," he mumbled, then yawned.

She put him back to bed and pulled the sheet over him.

"Don't leave," he said, opening his eyes and gazing at her in panic.

"I won't." She lay down beside him and felt him draw up into a circle, his back pressed into the curve of her side. Loving the son was as hard on the heart as loving the father, she thought. In a month or so, she'd be out of his life. He'd forget in time, but she wouldn't. She'd remember always.

She slept little during the night. Josh tossed and turned restlessly. She felt his forehead several times. At midnight, she slipped into the bathroom and got the digital thermometer.

She carefully inserted it into his ear. In a second, she had a reading. Josh had a temperature of 100.1 degrees.

He woke up. "Eden?"

"Here, darling."

He took her hand and clung to it.

"Are you feeling bad again?"

"I had a dream," he said. "I thought you were gone." He sighed wearily, wringing her heart, and was asleep once more.

At three, his temperature was 100.5. At four, it was 101.1. She called the doctor.

The pediatrician calmed Eden's fears. "Kids," she said in an amused tone. "It's probably from too much ice cream and cake, but if the pain intensifies or his temperature goes up another degree, let me know."

Eden sat in the rocker and kept watch. At five, Josh woke with tears streaming down his face.

"I hurt, Eden," he complained. "My head and my stomach."

As soon as she touched him, she knew his fever was higher. She quickly took it: 102.2 degrees.

"I feel sick," he said, wrapping his arms across his abdomen.

She called the doctor, who told her to go to the hospital emergency room. Eden threw on jeans and a top, then wrapped Josh in a sheet. She consulted with Henry, then carried Josh to her car. She arrived at the hospital ten minutes later.

The pediatrician met her and took Josh to the lab for some tests, while Eden filled out the admittance papers. When it came time to sign as parent or guardian, she hesitated, then put her name down. She called Mr. Remmick and told him what was happening.

"I'll be along shortly," he promised.

She hurried into the lab to be with Josh, who was throwing up into a basin when she entered. When he finished, he clung to her, his skin pale except for the fevered flush on his cheeks. He didn't seem to want to move.

The doctor returned in a few minutes. "We're going to prepare him for surgery," she said. "It's his appendix."

"He's so young," Eden protested.

Josh stirred a bit. "I'm six now," he reminded her.

"It's not usual in a child this age, but it's not all that rare, either." The doctor's smile was sympathetic. She touched

Josh, gaining his attention; then she told him what they were going to do. "Any questions?"

"Will it hurt?"

"Yes, but you'll be asleep. Afterwards, you'll be sore, and you'll have to take it easy for a few days. You'll have stitches."

"Neat. Kathy had stitches once. She hit her chin on some concrete." He didn't seem to think it sounded so bad.

The doctor gave him a shot, and he drifted into a doze. Then they took him from Eden's arms. The surgery was scheduled for two hours later, as soon as the surgeon finished with the patient he was working on. They put Josh to bed in a private room.

Eden called the house from the phone in there. Mr. Remmick and Henry were preparing to come to her, Mrs. O'Leary told her. "I've sent breakfast along," she added. "You'll need your strength."

Eden wished all of life's woes could be fixed with a hot meal and some TLC. But then, she admitted, a lot of them could.

When the door opened next, it wasn't Henry and Mr. Remmick who came in. It was Caleb.

Before they'd had time to exchange more than a glance, Josh threw off the sheet and tried to rise. She turned her attention back to him.

"Shh, lie still, love," she cautioned, smoothing the sheet.

"Eden," Josh mumbled. "Eden."

"I'm here."

She bent over him and ran a hand over his face. He wasn't as hot as he'd been earlier. Caleb came around to the other side of the bed. He took his son's hand.

"Hey, dude," he said. He gave the child a grave smile, but one that was filled with loving support and encouragement.

Eden felt the last of her anger melt as she witnessed the concern in Caleb's eyes and saw the weariness in the deepened lines of his face. He, too, had had a long night.

Josh opened his eyes and stared at his father, then his gaze shifted until he saw Eden. He stayed focused on her until his eyes began to drift closed again.

The door opened once more, and a young nurse bustled in with an IV unit. "Time for your final prep," she explained brightly. She smiled at Caleb. "If you'll move to the other side…"

He walked around the bed and stood behind Eden.

"Here," she said, realizing Caleb should be the one beside Josh. She stepped back to let him move closer.

Josh grabbed her with his free hand and held on. She saw the fear in his eyes.

"Josh, your father's here," she said, knowing Caleb needed to share this moment with his son, that he should be the one to hold and comfort the child. She tried to gently remove his hand.

The nurse, oblivious to the tension, took Josh's arm and wiped it with alcohol. "I'm going to tape your arm to this splint so you'll remember to hold it still," she explained. She strapped his arm, then picked up a needle from her tray in order to start the IV.

Seeing the needle, Josh let out a muted cry that tore at Eden's heart. He was trying so hard to be brave.

"Eden," he whimpered. "It hurts."

"I know, love. Soon you'll go to sleep, and when you wake, it'll be over."

"Will you be here all the time?" he asked.

"Yes. Your father and I will be right here."

Josh didn't glance at Caleb. He threw an arm around Eden's neck and clung to her. "I want *you*. Promise you'll stay," he pleaded. "You have to stay. Please."

"Of course," she murmured, holding him as the nurse finished taping the needle down and started the fluid dripping.

Eden caught a glimpse of Caleb's face. He looked as if he'd been stabbed. He swallowed once, then moved away and leaned against the wall, his expression impassive as he watched his son cling to Eden.

She wanted to explain that the child was frightened, that Josh hadn't meant to hurt him. It was just that he'd grown used to her taking care of him.

The nurse counted her patient's pulse, checked his temperature and blood pressure and then, giving them all a sympathetic smile, went to the door. "We'll be coming for him in ten minutes," she told them as she went out.

Josh buried his face in Eden's neck. "I want you to be my mother," he said. "I want to live with you."

Caleb left the room without a sound.

She stared after him, helpless to ease his pain when his son's need was so much greater.

Was it? her conscience questioned. *The boy is frightened. The man is in hell.*

He did it to himself. He was never there for Josh. I'm the one who cares about the child.

Caleb loves Josh, too.

But he's never available. He's always off on his trips. A person can't depend on him. Josh wants *me.*

He's Caleb's son.

He should have been mine!

He's Caleb's son.

But who will I have to love?

There was no answer.

Eden took a deep breath. "Josh, listen to me. Caleb… your father loves you very much—"

"No, he doesn't. He always goes away." Tears spilled over. "Are you going to leave me?"

"No," Eden assured him. "Neither is your dad. Give him a chance, Josh," she said sternly. "He traveled all night to get here. He wanted to be with you. He's trying to fix things so he can stay home with you from now on. Grandfather Remmick told me so. I know it's true."

Josh gave a hiccupy sniff and said nothing, but he was listening. He let go of her neck and relaxed. She saw that the medicine was taking effect. He was drifting into sleep. She had to talk fast.

"It's hard for some people to tell others that they love them. Your father is like that, so you have to help him. Tell him you love him. Tell him how you feel. He needs you to show him how to open up and be close to others. He's alone and hurting because he thinks you don't want him. Let me go get him."

She waited while Josh thought it over. At last, he nodded. His young face, so much like his father's, was very earnest. "I'll try," he promised.

"Good. He'll feel better once he knows you still love him. I'll find him and bring him back." She hurried out.

Caleb was in the waiting room, gazing out the window at the early morning brightness. He looked weary in a way Eden had never seen before, as if his spirit had fled. She touched his arm, then dropped her hand when he turned to her.

"Josh wants to see you," she said, trying to be gentle with this strong, independent man who didn't know how to react when he ached, except to hold it all inside.

Caleb shook his head. "He has you." A sad smile briefly touched his mouth. "You're all anyone ever needed."

"He needs *you*."

"I've lost him, Eden. You warned me but…" He shrugged, his eyes a fathomless well of misery. "It's too late."

"No, it isn't."

"You shouldn't feel sorry for me. I deserve—"

"I don't feel sorry for you," she snapped. "You're doing enough of it on your own. Your son is waiting for you, trying to stay awake so he can tell you he loves you. The least you can do is go to him and listen."

Caleb stared at her. He looked toward the hall.

"Go!" she ordered.

He took a step, looked at her, then caught her hand and pulled her down the hall with him. They went into Josh's room.

Releasing her, Caleb went to the side of the bed. Gingerly, he bent and put his arms on the bed on either side of Josh. They spoke at the same time.

"I love you, Josh."

"I love you, Dad."

Eden saw a sight she'd never seen. Just before he hugged his child, she saw tears in Caleb's eyes. She quietly left.

Sitting on the sofa in the waiting room, she experienced a fatigue that had nothing to do with her body. It was of the soul.

She'd done the right thing, she reminded herself. But it had been difficult. By giving Caleb his son, she'd given up her place in Josh's heart and his life. In so doing, she'd given up a chance at a place in the father's, too.

She could have had them both, father and son, and marriage, too. She could have continued to be the link between them, keeping the peace between them as Josh grew into a person with his own opinions and agenda for life.

But Josh was Caleb's son, not hers.

The boy was going to make a fine man. He would have his father's strengths, his charming ways. There was gentleness in Josh. And love. She thought they'd be all right now.

Picking up the Bible on the table beside her, she remembered that of all the people of Israel who had wandered for years in the desert, only Joshua and Caleb of the original group had been allowed into the promised land.

Only two of them, she thought. Not three.

Chapter Ten

Eden and Caleb waited, their nerves stretched taut, while Josh was in the operating room. The big hand of the clock inched around once, and then a bit more.

"Do you want a cup of coffee?" Caleb asked, the same question he'd asked not more than five minutes before.

"No," she said again.

A man in green surgical gear came to the door. They leaped to their feet. Eden felt Caleb's hand close on hers.

"He's in recovery and doing fine. No problems," the surgeon told them. "Got it before it burst."

"Thank God," Caleb muttered fervently.

"Yes," the doctor agreed with a smile. He listened to a page that came for him over the public-address system, nodded to them and walked out.

A nurse came in, the same one who'd inserted the IV. "Your son will be in recovery for an hour or so. Why don't you get something to eat? Believe me, you'll need your strength when he wakes up. Children always know when their parents are soft touches." She gave them an impish grin and left.

"Come on," Eden said to Caleb. "You look like death warmed over. Let's get that coffee you mentioned earlier."

Caleb called home and told his father the good news; then he and Eden went to the cafeteria and had a hot breakfast. They lingered at the table over their coffee.

"Do you think Josh will remember what we said before he went into surgery?" he asked.

"I'm sure he will," she replied.

She heard her voice as if from a distance. She sounded wise and calm and reassuring—her best schoolteacher manner. She glanced at Caleb, then away. He saw too much sometimes, especially where she was concerned.

In these moments of peace for him, knowing his son was safe, she didn't want to add the plangent note of her own sorrow. A month, she thought. Enough memories for a lifetime.

"Eden," he said.

"Yes?"

"Thank you."

She looked at him, a question in her eyes.

"It was your doing. You gave my son back to me. I… Words are inadequate, but…thank you."

She shook her head. "Your love was the key," she said softly. "Your love for your son, his love for you."

"Love is always the key, isn't it?" he mused aloud.

No answer was necessary, and she didn't bother with one. She couldn't have spoken, anyway. Her emotions were too shaky.

They returned to Josh's room. Fifteen minutes later, the nurses brought him in. He woke briefly when they moved him onto his bed. He glanced from Eden to his father, then gave them a weary smile before dozing off once more.

After the nurses left, Eden stayed where she was while Caleb moved toward the bedside. He stopped and, reaching out, pulled her to her feet. With an arm around her waist, he propelled her into place beside him. Together they stood looking down at the sleeping child.

"You were right," he said quietly. "A child is a gift, a living miracle." He looked out the window. "More than just a continuation of the species, a child is the promise of life, like a rainbow after the rain."

"Yes," she said huskily, unable to say more as the tears clogged her throat. When she moved away, he let her go.

Eden rested her novel on her stomach and watched Josh in the pool. He was swimming back and forth at a leisurely pace. This was his first day in the water since his operation almost three weeks ago. He was healing rapidly, but she didn't want him to overtax his strength.

She stretched and yawned, then gazed at the blue bowl of the sky. September. School would be starting in two weeks.

If only she could hold the minutes back, make them pass more slowly…make them last.

But of course, she couldn't. The most fervent of wishes couldn't stop the steady march of time. Tears clouded her eyes, but only for an instant. She refused to let herself cry.

She'd gone into this job with her eyes wide open and her heart securely locked out of harm's way. So she had thought.

What she hadn't figured into the equation was a little boy with mischief in his eyes and trust in his heart, she acknowledged. Nor the stubbornness of her own foolish heart in loving a man who didn't love her.

The sound of the patio door drew her attention.

Caleb walked out of the house. She hadn't heard his car, but he must have arrived some time ago. He'd changed from his business clothes to a bathing suit. He looked tanned and fit, his body taut with muscles that rippled smoothly when he walked to the side of the pool. He gave her a smile, then dived in.

"Dad!" Josh yelled when he heard the splash. He broke into a big grin.

Caleb swam toward his son. "How's it going?"

"Fine." Josh threw his arms around his father's neck and gave him a kiss.

Eden smiled as Caleb returned the gesture. He was getting better at showing his feelings, she thought. She rose from the lounge chair. She was getting better at hiding hers.

"I'm going to shower and dress," she called. "Don't stay in too long."

Two pairs of dark eyes, so very alike, turned to her.

"I'll watch the time," Caleb said. He watched her leave the pool area. The familiar heat attacked his insides. He wished he had the right to go in and shower with her.

"Eden doesn't like us anymore," Josh announced sadly.

"What?" Caleb stared at his son.

"It's true." The boy sighed heavily.

Caleb observed the misery in his son's expression. What had the child seen that he'd missed?

"Maybe we'd better talk about this," Caleb suggested. He rolled to his back in the water and headed for the shallow end of the pool. Josh swam along beside him.

After climbing out, they toweled off, then sat at the table with the big umbrella over it.

"What's this all about?" Caleb asked.

Josh gave him an unhappy look. "Haven't you noticed?" he asked in an aggrieved tone. "Eden doesn't do things like she used to. Things are different."

"What things?"

"Well, you know…like just now. She left us alone. And she didn't go sailing with us once this week."

Relief seeped through Caleb. "She's been getting her stuff ready for school, remember?"

"Yeah, but…she doesn't kiss me like she used to." A tinge of red crept into Josh's ears at this confession. "And sometimes she'd laugh and hug me, like if something was funny or we saw a red bird…things like that. But she doesn't anymore."

"Maybe she has a lot on her mind," Caleb suggested. He remembered how preoccupied he'd once been with his business deals. He'd hardly listened when Eden had chatted to him after his absences.

With a jolt of guilt, he realized he'd wanted only to hold her and make love to her for the scant amount of time he'd had between appointments. He wondered if she'd felt as if he saw her only long enough to satisfy his sexual appetites before he was off again on the real quests of his life. He bit back a groan.

For the past twenty days, he'd been at home. He'd found he could accomplish as much by using the phone or having the division managers fly in for a conference as he could by dashing around the world himself. He'd also discovered the quiet joy of having a home.

Caleb had asked Eden to stay at the house while Josh was recovering. She had agreed, although, now that he thought of it, there had been a reluctance on her part, a sort of panic in her eyes when she'd said yes.

Worried about his son, he'd backed off and given her room, thinking he was the problem and knowing that Josh needed her.

Sometimes he'd seen sadness in her eyes, he admitted, but he hadn't asked why. He'd tried to stay out of her way.

"Dad?"

Looking into his son's worried gaze, Caleb knew the time had come to have a talk with her…a serious talk. "I'll speak to her tonight and see if I can find out what's wrong."

Josh gave him a relieved smile. "Maybe she doesn't feel good. You know, like when I was sick. Maybe she needs an operation."

Caleb grinned and tousled Josh's hair. "I don't think it's that serious, but I'll see what I can find out, okay?"

"Okay." With that load off his mind, Josh asked his father if they could go fishing the next day. "With a picnic on the boat," he added. "Me and you and Eden."

"Sounds fun to me. I'll ask Eden when I talk to her."

"Great! Is it time for supper? I'm starved."

"Umm, we'd better get showered and changed," Caleb said, his mind on Eden. Standing, he started in.

He watched his son run ahead, slowing only at the steps and going up them a bit more cautiously than usual. Caleb felt a great squeezing sensation in the vicinity of his heart. He loved the child with a fierce protectiveness that some-times surprised him.

As he'd once loved Eden. He paused in the hall after Josh had disappeared into his room. As he still loved her.

He went into the master suite. The silence struck him. She should be there, humming while she dressed for dinner, her warm smile welcoming him….

A chill went through him. It might be too late. He may have waited too long before realizing the truth.

Eden stood by the window of the study, waiting for the others to appear. She had decided to go home the next day. She would come back to this house a few afternoons next week, then sort of fade out…like the sunset.

Josh no longer needed her. He had a full and busy life

with many friends. When school started, he'd never notice her absence.

"Bored?" A masculine voice spoke behind her.

"Nostalgic, I think," she said. She turned to Caleb, her smile carefully in place. She'd miss him and his autocratic ways, his endearing humor, even his temper. "The end of summer always makes me…" She couldn't find a word.

"Sad?" he suggested.

She shook her head, afraid to speak as emotion tightened her throat. She forced a calming breath and assumed her schoolteacher demeanor. "Not sad, but contemplative, perhaps. Autumn reminds me it's time to store away the memories of all those warm, lazy days in the sun and prepare for winter."

Winter, she reflected. She already felt the cold in her heart at the separation that was coming. She turned to the window and gazed out at the darkening landscape.

"I see." He walked over and stood behind her. They watched the fiery colors of the sunset in silence for a moment.

Eden was aware of him in every way—his warmth, the scent of his spicy cologne, the sound as he drew a deep breath, the release as he let it out in a heavy sigh that stirred the hair at her temple. He was much too close for her peace of mind.

"What's wrong?" he asked.

She glanced at him over her shoulder, then away. Much, much too close. "Wrong? Nothing."

"Eden—"

"Hi, Grandfather," Josh said in the hall.

When he came into the study with Mr. Remmick, his eyes darted from his father to her, Eden noted. There was a question in them. From the corner of her eye, she saw Caleb shake his head slightly.

They went into the dining room. Eden realized, with a

sinking of her heart, that this was probably her last meal with all three of the Remmick men at one time.

"How's the house coming along?" Mr. Remmick asked.

"I spoke to Mother this afternoon. The painters will be finished tomorrow." Eden laughed softly and glanced at Caleb. "She's pleased that she didn't have to do the work."

She saw Caleb's gaze glide over her face, stop at her mouth, then flick up to her eyes. Her breath shortened at the intensity in his perusal of her. She broke the contact.

When winter came, she thought, she'd have the memories of this summer to warm her. But she'd miss him.

There was no need to be despondent, she admonished herself. Life had a way of working out, if a person could only hold out through the rough times.

The summer hadn't been without its triumphs, she reflected. Josh and Caleb were growing closer each day. She felt she'd had a hand in that. Josh had made friends and was happy in his new environment. She'd helped there, too.

Like Mary Poppins, she had accomplished her primary goals. It was time to move on. She sighed and faced the loneliness she felt inside. She doubted if it would ever go away.

She realized everyone was looking at her. "I beg your pardon? I was woolgathering."

"Josh wants to know if you'll come sailing with us tomorrow," Caleb said. "We'll take a lunch and picnic somewhere—"

"I don't think so," she quickly cut in. She didn't think she could face having another day with them added to her memories. "I'm going home in the morning."

When she glanced at Caleb, she saw fury sweep into his eyes like a storm rushing in over the Great Lakes—fierce and wild and lethal. A tremor ran through her.

A tense silence fell, then Mr. Remmick asked Josh about the elementary school he would attend. Josh had taken part in an orientation day during the week.

"It's neat," Josh said. "Kathy will be in my class. And Rick Crenshaw. He's okay."

At a question from Caleb, Josh explained that Rick was the swimmer who had taken the blue ribbon at the swim meet, beating him out by a fraction of a stroke.

"Rick and me—"

"Rick and I," Eden and Caleb corrected together. She glanced at him, then away.

"Rick and I are going to practice together every day."

After the meal, they went into the study to relax before bedtime. Josh and his grandfather played chess. Eden read a novel. Caleb looked over a report.

When Josh went to bed, Caleb read to him, then called Eden to say good-night. Josh threw his arms around her and hugged her as tightly as he could. "Love you," he whispered into her hair.

For a second, she couldn't speak. "Love you, too," she finally managed. When she straightened up, Caleb was watching her with a narrow-eyed scrutiny that made her feel as if her heart were laid bare on a rock, ready for sacrifice.

Don't get melodramatic, she chided herself. She had a bad case of self-pity, that was all. She left the room.

Caleb caught up with her at her bedroom door. "I think I'll say good-night now," she told him. Her voice had only a slight catch in it.

"Not yet," he said. "I want to talk to you."

He started down the steps without looking back. She could almost see an aura of anger around him. What had she done?

The study was empty. Caleb shut the door after she was inside. He strode across the room and back, then stopped directly in front of her. She withdrew a pace.

"What's wrong?" he demanded.

She was taken aback by the question. "Why, nothing. Not with me. Is something…do you think something is wrong?"

"Hell, yes," he snapped. He stared into her eyes, as if he could look into her soul. "Why are you leaving?"

"Well, I…it's time," she explained hesitantly. "I mean, Josh is doing fine now. He doesn't need me, especially since you're home every night. It's time…."

Caleb towered over her, his eyes blazing. She faltered in her defensive explanation and stared at him.

"Why are you withdrawing?"

She searched the question for hidden meanings, but couldn't figure out the nuances. Weariness descended on her. She was too tired to deal with Caleb and his unpredictable moods. Since his return, he'd hardly spent a minute alone with her. Now he seemed furious because she was planning on returning to her own home.

"I'm not." She managed a smile. "What makes you think that?"

"Josh asked me today why you didn't do things with us. He thinks you don't like us anymore."

"How—how silly," she said, a tremor entering her voice.

Caleb moved closer, crowding her against a chair, which stopped her retreat. Danger signals flashed inside her. She tried to move to the side, but he reached out and grasped the chair back, trapping her within the confines of his arms.

"Is it?" he asked on a quieter note.

His tone had deepened, becoming husky, the way it used to when they made love. A frisson of longing ran through her. He leaned closer, so close she felt his breath fan lightly over her forehead and cheek as she turned her head.

"Don't you like us anymore, Eden?" he persisted in a near whisper, taunting her now.

She looked at him. A mistake. His lips were no more than three inches from hers. She drew a shaky breath and tried to assume her wise-teacher facade. "Really, Caleb, this is not a topic I care to pursue. I don't know what your problem is—"

"You." He leaned forward until his chest brushed hers. "You're my problem. What shall I tell Josh? That you don't care for him?"

"Of course not!" She slipped her hands between them, denying herself the pleasure of his warmth against her, then felt his heat penetrate her palms and seep through the rest of her body. Her knees softened like hot candle wax. "I love Josh very much."

"What about me?" he asked, his voice dropping to a lower register. "You love the son. How do you feel about the father?"

That brought her upright. She gave him a resentful glare. "Really, Caleb, I've had enough of this nonsense."

She pushed against his chest, but to no avail. He eased against her until their stomachs and thighs touched, too.

"You think I haven't?" he demanded, with a sudden return to anger. His hands moved so fast, she didn't realize what was happening. He cupped her face, bringing her lips perilously close to his. "I've given you as much space as I can. I've kept my distance since Josh came home from the hospital. But no more."

His mouth crashed down on hers. She tried to protest, but his tongue invaded, thrusting deep into her mouth. The hot longing of intense passion ran through her like a flash fire.

She raised her hands, but couldn't push him away. Instead, she gripped his shoulders and held on as desire ran rampant through her, melting any denial she would have made.

His hands slipped through her hair, down onto her back, then around her waist, pulling her closer, and closer still. She felt the hard pulsing of his body against hers and knew of his desire.

With an effort, she struggled against the overpowering surge of love she felt for him. Doing so was useless.

The kiss lasted through an eternity or two, until neither of them could catch a breath. He released her mouth and rested his cheek against her forehead.

"Eden," he said with a low groan.

"Caleb, let me go." She was near tears. She had to get away to the privacy of her room. Her control had shattered with the hard urgency of his kiss.

"No."

"Please."

"No." He shuddered against her and held her tighter. "Don't ask it of me, Eden. I can't let you go. Not now."

She moved her head helplessly from side to side, denying the hunger in him and the love in her. "Don't," she pleaded. "Don't. You're making this so hard for me."

He raised his head and stared into her eyes. "You think it isn't hard for me? You think I can just watch you walk out of my life, out of my son's life, without a word?" He gave her a little shake. "Well, I can't," he said grimly.

She lifted a shaking hand to brush a strand of hair away from her face. Confusion filled her. "What do you want from me?"

"Everything," he growled, the anger returning to his eyes, mixing with the passion she saw there.

"No!" She pushed against him, desperate to escape the lure of his embrace.

"Don't freeze up on me. You made me fight for my son at the hospital. You wouldn't let me give up on his love.

Follow your own teachings. If you want me, then show me. Fight for me, dammit. Show me you want me."

Ducking under his arm, she backed away from him, never taking her eyes from his as he followed in a ruthless stalking of her, frightening in his intensity.

"I won't melt in your arms the way I did when we first met," she said, remembering the bitter lessons of the past. "I'm not that naive girl anymore, Caleb. I won't be your son's caretaker by day and your mistress by night."

He stopped as if struck.

"I'm going home…to my house. I'll spend the afternoons with Josh this next week. After that, he won't need me anymore."

The sudden smile on his face mocked her distress. "I'm not talking about you being my mistress, Eden. If you want the son, you have to take the father. I'm asking you to be my wife."

The silence sizzled between them. She pressed a hand to her mouth to still the cry that rose in her. Her mother's advice rang through her: *You can have all your heart desires if you'd only reach out….*

Reach out and take what Caleb offered? Should she?

Cold reality set in. Yes, she could make a place for herself in their lives. Josh loved her. Caleb desired her. She was tempted…so tempted.

But to live a life longing for Caleb's love would be futile. Worse, it could turn into bitterness. She closed her eyes against the demand in his.

"Well?" he asked softly.

She looked at him. "I—I don't know."

He clenched his fists, pivoted and walked toward the door. "Think about it," he requested in an oddly controlled tone. "We'll spend some time together…as a threesome, so you won't have to worry about my baser instincts getting out of control again. Then maybe you can decide. Will you come sailing with us tomorrow?"

She thought of all the reasons she shouldn't, then nodded.

He walked out.

She sank into a chair and clasped her hands tightly in her lap. She knew what she wanted, but did she dare reach out for it? Fight for him? She didn't understand what he was asking.

Once upon a time she'd taken everything Caleb had offered without question, filling her greedy heart with a love that didn't exist. But she wasn't nineteen anymore. She'd never be as young and trusting as she'd been then.

Eden smoothed the sunscreen onto her face, then replaced her sunglasses and hat. The wind was gentle, and the sailboat skimmed along the water like a sylph. The leisurely pace, the quiet, the sense of being far from her troubles conspired to soothe her soul.

For long minutes, she could pretend that all was well in her world. But when she looked at Caleb, an electric current would run through every nerve in her body and she would remember she had a decision to make that would change her life forever.

Caleb set the trim on the sail, then glanced her way. Their eyes met and held for a split second before she looked away.

After a tour up the shoreline, Caleb found a wooded cove and dropped the anchor. He and Josh fished while Eden read.

An hour passed.

"I don't think they're going to bite today," Caleb said.

"Yeah," Josh agreed in a man-to-man tone.

Eden looked up and smiled. Her heart did a flip-flop as

she watched the two of them. She loved them with every ounce of love there was in her. She couldn't bear not to be the one who watched Josh grow into manhood, nor could she stand the thought of Caleb with another woman.

She closed her book and gazed at a tanker slowly making its way toward the city. She was going to accept Caleb's proposal. There really wasn't any other choice.

At noon, they opened the lunch Mrs. O'Leary had prepared for them. When Caleb handed her a sandwich, their fingers touched. Eden experienced the contact as a flow of electricity between them. He glanced at her, and she knew he felt it, too.

Yes, she thought, answering a question in her own mind. She couldn't live the rest of her life without him. She'd take what the gods were offering and not look back.

An unexpected peace descended on her.

After the meal, they hauled in the anchor and returned to the boat slip without incident. Josh held her hand as they walked up the steps to the parking lot. He opened the car door and slipped into the back seat before she could. Caleb held the front door for her.

On the way to the house, she noticed a woman in the car next to them at a stoplight looking them over. When the woman saw she had Eden's attention, she smiled ruefully.

Eden realized the woman was envious of her. She and Caleb and Josh looked like a family. She glanced around at the two men. Josh and Caleb were planning a trip to the zoo for the next afternoon. They were laughing, their identical dark eyes filled with mirth as Caleb told a story of a spitting camel.

"Green spit? Neat!" Josh exclaimed. "I'd like to see that."

"Gentlemen, please," Eden said.

Caleb reached over and brought her hand to his lips. He kissed the back of her fingers and released her. "Ladies have delicate ears, Josh. We men have to watch our language in front of them."

Josh giggled. "Eden has eaten alligator steak, Dad. She told me so."

"Hmm, pretty tough, huh?" Caleb gave her a teasing glance.

Eden wanted to tell him he didn't have to be so charming and thoughtful—she'd decided to marry him. She'd wait until they were alone. Tonight. After everyone was asleep.

The twilight seemed to drag its feet as it ambled into night. At last Josh was in bed, after kissing her and his father good-night twice each. Mr. Remmick left the study a half hour later. She and Caleb were alone. She cleared her throat.

"Would you like a glass of wine?" Caleb asked.

"Yes, please." While they were drinking it, she would tell him. Maybe. No, she would.

He poured each of them a glass of red wine and took the chair next to the sofa where she sat. He raised his glass to her before taking the first sip. She returned the silent toast.

Her eyes were caught by his. He gazed into them as he drank. The peace brought on by her decision to accept the inevitable wavered a bit. She drew it tightly around her like a protective cloak. "Uh," she said nervously, trying to get the words out.

She couldn't approach it baldly, like a business contract, she found. Marriage was an intimate merging, not an arrangement.

Caleb rose and resettled himself on the sofa beside her. He set his glass on the coffee table. "You seem to have something on your mind."

A sigh of relief escaped her. "Yes."

"Me, I hope." He moved closer to her. "Not to sound vain, but I've noticed you watching me all day."

Heat flared in her cheeks. She took a sip of tart wine, then set the glass aside. Her hands trembled slightly. They were cold when she clasped them together.

"I've watched you, too." He slipped his hand into her hair, holding her still while he nuzzled his nose against her. "Josh was happy today. So was I. The best day I've had in ages. Did you enjoy it?"

"I…yes." Her heart was pounding so loudly, she thought he could surely hear it. "Caleb," she whispered. "What are you doing?"

He turned her face to his and smiled lazily at her. "Can't you tell?"

She shook her head.

He bent and kissed her surprised mouth. "Open for me," he murmured, biting at her lips.

"No."

He explored her mouth with his tongue, slowly, thoroughly. She laid a hand on his arm and held on. When he raised his head, his eyes blazed with passion, yet he kept his touch gentle, as if banking the desire.

"I'm wooing you," he said; then he kissed each corner of her mouth and ran his tongue over her lips, savoring the taste.

A shudder of pure longing went through her. She pushed him away. "You don't have to," she said. "I've decided to accept."

She sounded as prim as the proverbial spinster.

He frowned at her, absorbing the impact of her words; then he heaved himself off the sofa, kicked a hassock out of his path and stomped to the broad window. He gripped the frame while she stared at his back, totally confused.

"I'll marry you," she clarified, in case he hadn't understood.

He hit the wood framing with the heel of his fist. A tremor of fear plunged through her.

"If you still want to," she added.

Caleb spun around. "Why?"

She spread her hands helplessly. "Well, there's Josh. I truly care for him."

"And me?" His voice was hoarse, as if the words were torn from him. "Do you truly care for me?"

"Yes," she managed to say. She closed her eyes. He wanted the truth; he would get it. "I—I..." She couldn't say it.

He moved then, swiftly descending on her. She felt herself lifted; then she was in his lap. She opened her eyes and blinked against the tears that insisted on forming.

"Do you really care for me at all?" he asked. "Is there a chance for us? God, Eden, tell me. I'm dying inside."

"Caleb?" She touched his brow, then ran a shaky hand into his black, unruly hair.

Caleb caught her face between his hands. "I love you," he whispered fiercely. "I've never stopped. You're my soul, my life. Without you, I'm dead inside. Without you...life has been an unending hell. For years...*years*. You've got to love me again, the way you used to, with everything in you, no holding back. I'll fight for that love, Eden, I won't stop until you're mine."

He kissed her then, hot, sweet, tempestuous kisses all over her face and neck. His hand searched under her blouse until he caressed her skin. A groan of need escaped him.

He could feel her trembling against him, her hands, even her mouth almost shaking with the force of her emotion. He closed his eyes and let the love sweep over him.

"I need you," he told her.

"Yes," she whimpered against his lips. "Yes."

He pressed her back against the sofa, letting her slide off

his lap, then turning so he lay partially over her, her legs over his. He laid a hand on her breast and felt her heart pounding.

"Say it," he ordered.

She heard the plea. "I love you. I've never stopped."

"Ah, love." He kissed her wildly, his hands creating havoc wherever he caressed.

The door opened. Josh walked in, rubbing his eyes. He stopped when his two favorite adults looked up at him.

Eden tried to scoot away, but Caleb held her in an unbreakable grip. He smiled at his son.

"Are you going to get married?" Josh demanded.

Caleb nodded.

The two males grinned at each other.

Eden looked from one to the other. "I think this has been discussed before," she said.

"Yes," Caleb admitted. He saw the uncertainty in her eyes. "My son and I both love you like mad. Both of us," he repeated firmly, so she would know he meant it.

"Right," Josh said.

Caleb straightened and held out his arm to his son. Josh dived onto the sofa with them. Caleb held them both in a bear hug.

"We really love you," Josh told Eden.

"I love you, too," she echoed. "Both of you."

Caleb saw the tears in her eyes. He saw the happiness. Most of all, he saw the love. He kissed them—his son and his woman.

Chapter Eleven

Caleb paid the taxi and headed for the door, pulling his tie off as he went. He was in a hurry.

The cool house welcomed him, dissolving some of the stress of Chicago in late July. He tossed his briefcase onto a chair, his coat and tie after it, then headed for the pool.

Josh was there, patiently showing three-year-old Amanda how to improve her swimming stroke, which was mostly a dog paddle. She squealed when she saw him.

"Daddy, Daddy. Daddy's home! Momma, Daddy's home."

Caleb grinned. He knelt and waited as his son, daughter and the family dog—all three trailing water—rushed toward him. He gathered them in his arms, not caring that his shirt and pants soon became soggy. Across the garden, he saw his father and Henry coming toward the house, aware that he was home.

Home. God, it felt good.

He looked around with a little frown. There was one thing missing…. He spotted Eden at the kitchen window, smiling at him through the glass. She pursed her lips and blew him a kiss.

"Excuse me, kids. Mom needs some attention."

He pushed the kids and the dog off his lap after giving them each one more kiss and accepting a welcoming lick on his chin. He stood and waved to his father, then headed for the kitchen.

Eden was scraping batter into a cake pan. She wore a one-piece swimsuit, cut high, that showed off her long, beautiful legs to perfection. He closed his arms around her and nuzzled her neck. She laughed and shook her hair out of the way, encouraging him.

"I've missed you," he murmured, kissing her ear.

"It's only been one day," she reminded him.

"A thousand years," he corrected. "I want you."

She put the bowl in the sink and added water. He went with her when she crossed the kitchen to put the cake in the oven, not letting her out of his arms. As soon as she closed the oven door, he turned her around and kissed her on the mouth, taking his time, savoring the sensations.

"We have forty minutes," she murmured when he let her up for air. "Dad and Henry will watch the kids."

He was tempted. "Later. I want lots of time and no rushing." He kissed her again, then let her go. "I'll change into my trunks."

When he rejoined them, Eden and the children, including the dog, who thought he was one of the them, were in the pool. He played tag with them until dark.

After baths and dinner, Caleb read to his daughter until she was sleepy, then went in to tell his son good-night. Josh, who had a later bedtime, was reading to himself.

"Dad?" he said on a worried note, a shy manner about him.

"Yeah, Son?" Caleb sat on the side of the bed.

"Dad, when you like someone, *really* like someone, do you feel all sort of funny inside? Almost…sort of… hurting, like your stomach gets all painful?"

For a minute, Caleb remembered how he'd felt the first time he'd laid eyes on Eden. "Yeah, that's exactly it."

They sat there in silence for a minute.

"Chris?" Caleb asked. Josh had had a crush on her for years.

Josh grimaced. "Nah, she's *old.*"

"Hmm," Caleb said.

"It's…uh…well, Kathy is pretty neat, you know. Don't tell Mandy, okay? She'd just blab everything." His ears turned red.

Caleb felt his heart contract at the shared secret. *Ah, Eden, my love, you gave me these—the moments in my children's lives.* "Okay," he said lightly. "Kathy is a fine person."

"Yeah. You ever notice she's like Eden?"

"Is she?"

"Umm-hmm. You still love Eden a lot, don't you?"

"Totally, with funny pains in my stomach and everything."

The two males exchanged understanding glances. Josh sighed happily. "Good. She was afraid you'd be mad. She scraped the fender on your new car this morning."

"I'll kill her," Caleb said, rising.

Josh caught his hand. "Be careful. I think she's having another baby."

Caleb started, then ruffled his son's bangs. "Men are always gentle with women." He kissed his son on the forehead and went to find his wife…in case there was something the little sneak wanted to tell him.

He found her in their room, humming while she brushed her hair. She gave him a sexy glance in the mirror.

Dropping to his knees in front of her, he put his arms around her hips. "Josh thinks you're going to have a baby."

She laughed. "No, Charlie is."

"Charlie," he repeated blankly. "The dog? But she was supposed to have been fixed. Sue said— That blasted Sue," he concluded ominously.

"I think she told us that so we'd take the animal for the summer." She leaned over and kissed him. "Would you mind if we were to have another?"

His eyes darkened when he looked into her face. He forgot all about dogs and scraped fenders. "Mind? Not as long as I get to help make 'em." He raked her with a slow grin, removed the brush from her hand and put it aside, then pulled her to her feet. He removed the gown and led her to the bed. There, he tossed aside his jeans and shirt and joined her, pulling her close.

She lifted her mouth eagerly to his, taking his passion, taking all he could give and giving it back with interest. He kissed her a thousand times and told her of his love.

"It's almost worth it to leave home," he murmured, "knowing I get to come back to you." But he was rarely gone, and never overnight if he could help it. He still liked making deals and watching plans he'd conceived being put into motion, but there were other things in life, things that made the rest worth it.

She held his face between her hands. "Yes. Come to me," she whispered, kissing him. "Come to me now."

He did, eager to show his love for her in all the ways he knew. "I brought you a present. It's in my briefcase," he remembered to tell her.

"I like this one best." She closed her eyes and moved against him, holding him, giving him joy, giving him life.

Later, when she was asleep, he wondered if she'd re-membered that today would have been their eleventh wedding anniversary if they'd married the first time. Instead, it was only their fourth. Seven years wasted. No, not wasted, he amended, thinking of Josh.

Eden and Josh and Amanda—our Mandy—as they called the feisty youngster.

His family.

He remembered lines from a poem, "Home is the sailor, home from the sea / and the hunter home from the hill," and knew he was where he belonged.

Yes.

* * * * *

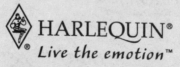

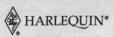

Invites *you* to experience lively, heartwarming all-American romances

Every month, we bring you four strong, sexy men, and four women who know what they want—and go all out to get it.

From small towns to big cities, experience a sense of adventure, romance and family spirit—the all-American way!

Love, Home & Happiness

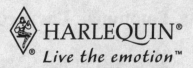

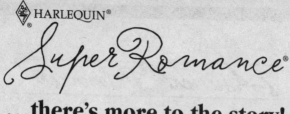
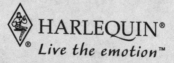

HARLEQUIN®
INTRIGUE®

BREATHTAKING ROMANTIC SUSPENSE

Shared dangers and passions lead to electrifying romance and heart-stopping suspense!

Every month, you'll meet six new heroes who are guaranteed to make your spine tingle and your pulse pound. With them you'll enter into the exciting world of Harlequin Intrigue— where your life is on the line and so is your heart!

THAT'S INTRIGUE— ROMANTIC SUSPENSE AT ITS BEST!

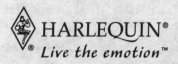

HARLEQUIN®
Live the emotion™

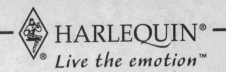

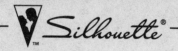

SPECIAL EDITION™

Emotional, compelling stories that capture the intensity of living, loving and creating a family in today's world.

Silhouette

Desire

Modern, passionate reads that are powerful and provocative.

Silhouette

nocturne

Dramatic and sensual tales of paranormal romance.

Silhouette Romantic

SUSPENSE

Romances that are sparked by danger and fueled by passion.